Quill's Adventures

in Grozzieland

John Waddington-Feather
Illustrated by Doreen Edmond

John Muir Publications
Santa Fe, New Mexico

First published 1988 by Feather Books, England

John Muir Publications, P.O. Box 613, Santa Fe, NM 87504

Second edition. First printing

Library of Congress Cataloging-in-Publication Data
Waddington-Feather, John, 1933-
    Quill's adventures in Grozzieland / John Waddington-Feather. —
2nd ed.
        p.   cm.
    Summary: Quill Hedgehog and his friends from the Great Beyond try
to thwart the plan to blot out the sun and moon that alley cat Mungo
Brown has devised with the help of the underground Grozzies in order
to take over the world.
    ISBN 1-56261-017-1
    [1. Hedgehogs — Fiction.   2. Conservation of natural resources —
Fiction.]   I. Title.
PZ7.W11375Qu   1991
[Fic] — dc20   91-22512
                                                                      CIP
                                                                        AC

Designer: Marcy Heller
Typeface: Trump Mediaeval and Hadriano Roman
Typesetter: Business Graphics
Printer: Banta Company

Distributed to the book trade by
W. W. Norton & Company, Inc.
New York, New York

Doreen Edmond

To Sarah, Katherine and Anna,
for whom this tale was first told

Foreword

Those of you who've read the earlier Quill Hedgehog stories will recognise certain Humanfolk features in some of the Animalfolk. It's bound to happen when we share the same world. We pick up the good and the bad from each other, and only each one of us can decide what's good and what's bad, what to keep and what to drop. Poor, old Mungo Brown always seemed to keep the bad and drop the good.

The Grozzies had done much the same thing. They'd once been very bright people. But they'd become so superior, so full of themselves, they saw little of what was good outside their own ideas of the world. If we, too, look only at our own ideas and nobody else's, there's a danger the good in us will die and the bad grow. We feed on the worst part of ourselves—just as fungus grows on dead things.

As it happened, the Grozzy commanders, men of rank in their world, had very high-sounding names; but they were names of an unpleasant sort of fungus, woodrot! Daedalia Quercina, Poria Monticola, Coniophora Cerebella, and Merulius Lacrymans are all names for woodrot, which the four Grozzies had grown very like. Indeed, but for the effort of the Animalfolk, they'd have turned completely into fungus.

Perhaps there's a lesson there for all of us, if we don't listen to others, and if we cease to see anything wonderful in the world. It doesn't usually happen to young folk, but neither does woodrot appear in healthy, young wood. It's when you start growing up that you pick up bad ideas, so beware!

A NEW and ACCVRAT MAP of —

Scrobbescine   Ye Olde Ruins of Virocos

Nightshade Cottage (where Witches lived)

Ye Hides where ye Animalfolk observed ye Humanfolk
Ye Caves where Tobias Toad
& ye others hid

Magna Mere

Islands
Webfoot Island

Ye Great Mere of Mellowmark
Under which was ye
Olde Grozzielande
Ye Mystery Marsh
Ye Old Tunnal
Ye Black Wood
Domusland
Tha Lythe

Ye Police Station
(of Mick & Mack &
Pip Fieldmousa)

Ye Standing Hills

Ye Highway where Bert Squirrels
Horse bolted

Dormouse
Dingle
Ye Great Oak

Performed by Doreen Edmond and
to be found by John Muir Publications
cum Privilegio Santa Fe.

Ye Hedgehog
Meadow
(where Quill lives)

Ye Eelbrook

15 of ye Animalfolk Leagues

Neron Islet

Over There

Ye Wind Sea

Chapter 1

Nero Squinks, Elderman Nero Squinks, to give him his full title, the one-eyed rat who'd made good after half a lifetime's shameless wrongdoing, certainly had turned over a new leaf. In fact, not only had he turned over the shady side of his particular leaf to start a new chapter in his life-book but he'd encouraged others in Wasteland to follow his example. As a result their land was transformed. Gone were the spoilheaps and mountains of slag. Gone were the filthy waterways and broken dams. Gone were acres of mean houses which once housed mean folk in mean cities. Gone, indeed, were the cities themselves. Collections of little villages appeared in their place as a new land appeared.

It was a green and pleasant land, a land where farming revived, where crops were grown and flocks appeared in living fields. Long grey-veined walls straggled once more down the Misty Mountains, enclosing new sheep in new pastures. They changed into the green arteries of hedgerows when they met the plains, and these in turn merged with new woodlands. Trees grew where they hadn't grown for years, and along the Misty River, young Wastelanders began to make weekend outings with fishing rods and jamjars, just as their great-great-great-great-grandfathers had done generations before. So ordered and peaceful did the

Wastelanders keep their country that its very name was changed . . . back to its ancient name, Mellowmark, after the great lines of stones which ran all round its borders, placed there many years before by long-lost folk of the olden days.

And for ten years, Mellowmark lived at peace with its neighbours—the Domuslanders across the Mystery Marshes, the Great Beyonders over the Staying Hills, and the Merefullians from Mereful in the east. But in the eleventh year of Nero's Eldermanship, odd things began to happen. If I told you that a year or two before Mungo Brown had been released from prison, you'll guess at once he had a dirty paw in the business, for he it was who'd caused all the trouble in the past.

After his overthrow as President of Wasteland, he'd been locked up in the same prison he'd kept Quill Hedgehog, Dink Dormouse, and the two magpies years before. They, as you'll remember, were freed by that daring raid in Hoot Owl's Hootacopter, which eventually led to Mungo's downfall. So, Mungo had been freed and expelled from Mellowmark to live no one knew where . . . until the beginning of this story.

Now Nero still visited the old mineshafts near the Mystery Marshes to practise his singing. From a very early age his mother had encouraged him to take up a career in music and he'd become a lifelong addict of grand opera, oratorio, folk music—anything, indeed, connected with song. Sadly, there were two drawbacks—he was no musician, and he couldn't sing. He possessed the most vicious pair of vocal chords nature had ever invented. We all know that sometimes nature goes wrong; but in creating Nero's voice box, she'd gone utterly astray.

When he sang it was like . . . well, it was like nothing on earth, but I'll make a stab at describing it. If you can imagine hundreds of raw fingernails being scratched across rough concrete walls, or countless sticks of chalk screeching drily over shiny blackboards, or numberless, unoiled doors creaking grimly on their desiccated hinges, all operating at the same time as a thousand hooters and a host of those infernal bells in school corridors which fracture the air as you pass beneath them, then you're only beginning to grasp what an unholy row Nero's larynx made when he began to tune up. It was diabolical!

In the old days he'd been banned from singing anywhere in Wasteland, except deep in the mines on its eastern side which ran under the Mystery Marshes. And it was when he'd gone on one of his singing sprees that he noticed something peculiar happening further down the mineshaft where he practised.

Nero knew the galleries there like the back of his paw. He knew where every shaft began and ended, where the coal-mines started and where the lead-mines interlinked with them further up the hillside. Yet one evening, when he'd gone to sing by himself after a rather hard day at Squinkstown Town Hall, he heard a noise through the wall of rock at the end of the tunnel he sang in.

He was about to nail his music to an old pit-prop, to stop the score blowing away when he tuned up, and he couldn't believe his ears. He paused to listen, this time more intently. Sure enough, after a short interval the noise began again, a sort of scrabbly, scrapy noise. Cautiously he tip-toed nearer the rockface and gave it a long, hard look. The strange noise continued, and he touched the surface gingerly. It seemed solid enough, yet he felt the smallest vibrations come through to the tips of his paw. There was something happening on the other side . . . something very, very strange!

Nero wasn't given to fanciful ideas like you and me. Although he'd turned over a new leaf and had become a model citizen, he still lacked imagination. He was a very down-to-earth rat, particularly when he practised singing. What's more, he'd nerves of steel. He had to have

3

otherwise he'd never had coped with the horror of his own voice. Yet a thought passed through his mind which sent cold shivers down his spine. That thought was 'Grozzy'—a word which terrified every Mellowmarkian.

It had the same effect on the Mellowmarkfolk that 'ghosts' or 'goblins' might have on you if you thought you were going to meet them. No one had actually seen a Grozzy, just as I suspect no one has ever seen a real ghost or goblin. Nevertheless, they were spoken about in Mellowmark with the same knowledgeable air that certain people discuss ghosts or goblins in our part of the world.

When all's said and done, just because we haven't seen a ghost or had the pleasure of being introduced to a goblin, that doesn't mean to say they don't exist. I've never seen Santa Claus fill my stocking on Christmas Eve, but it's always full on Christmas morning. So I'm certainly not going to stop believing in him at my time of life . . . what's more, my Christmas presents might stop if I did.

On the other hand, I sometimes wish I didn't believe in ghosts, because I've no wish to bump into one or walk through one, or whatever happens when one meets a ghost down dark lanes or in empty houses; for there are occasions when I have to walk down dark lanes and when I find myself at home alone.

But back to the Grozzies. These terrible creatures had been spoken about in Mellowmark ever since anyone had anything to speak about in that country. The Grozzies were as old as the Mellow Stones themselves; indeed, some knowing rats even went as far as saying they'd been put there by the Grozzies to mark out their territory.

Perhaps you're wondering what exactly Grozzies were like. Well, I'll tell you, for I've had dealings with creatures very like them myself. They were like Humanfolk in a primitive sort of way. Some of us to this day have Grozzy characteristics one way or another. I certainly

4

have, but I wouldn't want to be associated with them. They'd come from no one knew where, blundering as Humanfolk will do, into the world of animals and mucking it up way back in the olden days.

The Grozzies were supposed to be utterly bad. They'd mellowed a bit when this story opens, but they were still pretty anti-social by our standards. They'd gone into the depths of the earth thousands of years before simply because the sunlit world above had grown too beautiful for them. They'd become so wrapped up in their own sick world of misery and ugliness, no longer could they see anything of beauty outside, so they'd taken themselves off in a fit of sulks to live underground, live life as they wanted, complaining and grumbling all the time.

Grozzies still looked like Humanfolk after a fashion. They'd two long, hairy arms and short, bandy legs. Their bodies were covered with long black hair, and they wore skins of animals, mainly silly rabbits that had blundered into their caverns and got caught.

The most strange—and most terrible—thing about them was their eye, their one, solitary eye stuck right in the middle of their foreheads. It glowed dully in the perpetual dark of their caverns and was the only means of light down there. This terrible eye sent out a beam that paralysed anyone it fell upon. It made you a stage worse than groggy. It made you grozzy—hence their name. Once you'd been grozzified, you were carted off senseless back to their lairs, put into cold storage, then microwaved by that same terrible eye when the Grozzies felt hungry. Need I say more?

All this was hearsay, though it must have been based on fact. Most rumours are. But for generations no one had seen a Grozzy in Mellowmark, not distinctly; though there were several, elderly Mellowmarkians, whose families lived near the Mystery Marshes in the old cottages there, who swore on oath they'd seen creatures very like

5

Grozzies. They'd seen them on dark nights, wandering about in the marsh fogs, beaming their deadly beams this way and that as they prowled around.

One old rat, Codger Squeak, said he'd been grozzified way back in his youth. Fortunately for him, the clouds had parted just as a Grozzy was coming to pick him up and the moonbeam which fell on him saved him. No Grozzy will stay above the ground when it's light, even moonlight, and they'd scuttled back into the mines hissing and yammering in a most unpleasant way said Codger.

He'd been found by his dad next morning, still grozzified and unable to move. And so he'd remained for days till the wise Dorwoman, who lived over the border in Domusland, had been brought in to look at him. She knew a thing or two, did old Widow Dor, and her herbal dressing had brought Codger to his senses again.

He'd tried to tell his dad what had happened. He didn't believe him and went so far as to order him never to speak about it again. Nevertheless, Codger stuck to his story. He knew what had happened, and he wasn't going to change his story for anyone . . . not after he grew up, anyhow. And the older he got, the more he elaborated his tale. He could hold younger rats spellbound for hours telling of how he'd been grozzified at their age and what it felt like. The older rats claimed they didn't believe him. It was highly significant, though, that none of them would go out at night without a well-lit lantern. On very dark nights they didn't go out at all, but kept the darkness well outside behind locked doors.

Despite Codger Squeak's story and other tales which sprang up, Nero Squinks remained unmoved. As I said, he'd little imagination when it came to believing in things like Grozzies, though he'd once imagined his voice supreme. It was . . . supremely awful! Years before, when he'd gone down secretly to practise singing in the mines, the din he'd created was so ghastly it simply reinforced

6

folks' belief that there was something dreadful living down there in the abandoned pits. No decent creature could have made noises like that. And as the years went by, his singing not only drifted up . . . it seeped down. It reached the kingdom of the Grozzies and they didn't like it either, till finally they decided to come up and grozzify whoever it was kept them awake at nights.

So, we come back to the beginning of this story when Nero heard the peculiar noises on the other side of the rockface. As his paws felt the vibrations grow stronger and stronger, and as bits of dust and stone began crumbling down, he noticed a crack and through it a weird, red light appeared. There was a large boulder nearby, just under the crack, and he climbed it to look through. What he saw made his one eye grow wider and wider, but he said never a word. He was glued to the spot. He'd been grozzified!

Chapter 2

On the opposite side of the Mystery Marshes, in Domusland, lived two very good friends of Nero Squinks. They shared with Nero the happy experience of having turned over new leaves in their very colourful lives. It had been some chapters back in the book of their lives. In fact, a whole volume, for I'm sorry to say they'd once been burglars, very accomplished burglars, too. None of your hit and grab stuff. But that had been in younger, less responsible days; now they were models of virtue, patterns of good behaviour for every young Domuslander.

One was called Police Sergeant Mack the very Fat. The other had once been called Mick the Thin, but he was thin no longer. They were magpies and officers of law and order for the Black Wood Shire part of Domusland. The Moot had appointed them police constables there after the Wasteland adventure some years before.

In that adventure, they'd helped Quill Hedgehog and Dink Dormouse. They'd also met Nero Squinks then, but he was a very different person from the Nero in this story. It was the Nero of the bad old days, and they'd had a hand in his reform, which had made them great friends. So much so, that after singing his heart out under the earth each Friday night, Nero would take himself off to Domusland by a secret tunnel under the Mystery Marshes, to relax with his two friends at Black Wood Shire police station. There, over a box of chocs and something good in their glasses, they'd talk over old times and more recent ones.

It had become routine over the years. Friday night was music night for the hardworking Mayor of Squinkstown. After finishing his day's work, Nero would go for a sing, then cross to Domusland for the weekend with the Magpiefolk. Then he'd return to Mellowmark on the Sunday night ready for a week's work the next day. Rarely did he miss a weekend, and when he couldn't come, he always let the magpies know.

Great was the magpies' surprise when, on the night Nero was grozzified, he failed to appear. They'd have been even more surprised had they known what had happened! Surprise gave way to worry, and worry to fear that something had befallen Nero. He always came on time, being a most punctual rat. But they'd never been happy about his singing alone so deep in the mines. You see, they'd had the misfortune to actually hear him sing. He used to inflict his singing on the prisoners in Wasteland Gaol where they'd been locked up and Nero had been a warder.

They'd never heard him since . . . nor did they want to, but having heard him once, they feared his voice might dislodge the old pit-props and bring the place crashing down on him. However, this never happened. Nero examined them all at regular intervals . . . especially those in direct line with his voice, which had much the same effect as an artillery barrage when he struck up.

On the Saturday, the two birds decided they could wait no longer. They'd recently recruited a third member to the force, a young fieldmouse called Pip. He was keen and alert, as all police-cadets ought to be. He tried hard to reach the high standard of policing that Mick and Mack set him. However, hard as he tried, I doubt if he'd quite reach their superb level. You see, he'd never been a professional burglar like them, never taken exams in crime

Young Police-cadet Pip receives his instructions from Sergeants Mick and Mack Magpie

like many criminals I know, who, when they turn over new leaves, tend to have just that bit more expertise which leaf-overness gives you, when you start to earn an honest living.

As policemen, it helped them immensely to know what the opposition were up to; advantages burglars never dreamed of, so were caught red-handed. There wasn't a criminal in Domusland who could pull a fast one on Mack and Mick. In fact, after a while, there weren't any criminals at all. They were caught before they crimed!

The cells in their police station remained unoccupied for years. And that was a shame. Empty rooms should be filled, so Sergeant Mack decided to put the two cells to good use. One was used for growing mushrooms, and the other had its cell window removed and replaced with a large sheet of glass to make a pleasant conservatory. Rarely could a police station have looked so greenhousey or smelled so mushroomy.

"Well, my lad," said Mack to young Pip, as he put on his helmet. "We're going to Mellowmark to see what's happened to Elderman Squinks. Now make sure you look after everything and see there's no trouble while we're away. You know where all the books are kept and how to register anything lost or found. I don't expect we'll be long gone, but I want to come back and find all my plants watered and all my mushrooms picked and not gone weevilly. You understand?"

"Yes, sir," said young Pip, standing up very straight, as Mack flicked a speck of dust off his shoulders and fastened a top button the fieldmouse had left undone.

"An' I don't want to see you going around half-dressed either. Smarten yourself up a bit, my lad!" said the sergeant.

"Yes, sir," said Pip again, looking a little crestfallen. He tried so hard, and he took everything so much to heart that Sergeant Mack said.

The two magpies went out, and Mick slipped Pip a coin to buy a fizzy lemonade to cheer himself up. The fieldmouse brightened appreciably and quietly thanked Mick, peering through the window boxes on the station window ledge till the magpies were out of sight. Then he nipped across the road to Mrs. Flit's shop for his bottle of lemonade.

Mick and Mack made their way to the tunnel under the Mystery Marshes, a much smaller one than that which Hoot had blown up years before. At its entrance the two policemen looked for Nero's lantern, which he always left hanging. There was no sign of it. Clearly, he hadn't got that far, and they became more worried than ever. They switched on their belt lanterns and went in, cautiously.

They'd gone in scores of times and felt no qualms at all, but on this occasion there was a certain . . . a certain eeriness. Something they felt rather than understood. Something very akin to walking through a graveyard on a dark night.

"I say, Mick," whispered Mack, "do you feel anything different tonight about this place?" Why he was whispering he couldn't say, but for the life of him he daren't raise his voice. Nor did Mick.

"I don't know how to put it," said the other magpie in a fearful whisper, "but you're right. There's something odd, definitely odd in the air around here. If we'd been back at the station I'd have put it down to the mushrooms. But there ain't no mushrooms here . . . only their smell. And not exactly that . . . it's more of a fusty smell . . . more like toadstools."

"My own feelings to the letter," said Sergeant Mack, glancing warily around as they moved deeper and deeper into the shaft. "Most odd . . . most exceedingly odd . . . and I don't like the smell of it in every sense. It ain't appetising. It's off-putting . . . like toadstools as you say."

They trod cautiously down the tunnel, and at each step the fungus smell grew stronger. In time, they reached the place where Nero held his practices. All seemed normal except there was his music still nailed to its stand, and there was his candle snuffed out. In addition there was a tin whistle which he sometimes played to keep himself company when he rested his voice. Mick played the flute and picked it up. He couldn't resist giving a few notes on it, for he was quite an accomplished flautist. It proved their undoing!

After the first couple of bars, the strange light Nero had seen reappeared. It grew stronger, and Mick stopped playing. He put the whistle in his pocket, and he and Mack started to back away, but it was too late. They were surrounded. The Grozzies' beams were on them, and they stood bewitched, frozen to the spot. Cold, clammy hands turned off their lights as Mack yelled, "Goodness gracious! Grozzies!" It was the last thing he said for some time, for as the light from the Grozzies' eyes fell upon him, he like Mick was grozzified.

The Grozzies were delighted. They squeaked and spluttered no end. They had a bad habit of pronouncing their esses in a very disturbing way. It put you off them at once, and the magpies were more than put off. They were put away. The Grozzies picked them up and carried them to their kingdom, hissing and snickering most horribly in triumph. They began to sing a dull marching-song as they stomped down the tunnel into the depths of the earth:

"Success! Success!
Our king has brought success!
Mealsies, suppersies by the score
Marching through our larder door,
King Mungo brings us more and more
Success upon success!"

Each time they completed this dreary victory-song they gave three wet, Grozzy cheers all the way to Grozzieland. They hissed and spat so energetically, they sounded like a pit of sneezing vipers and made the magpies go cold all over.

It seemed an age they marched down that tunnel . . . down, down, down. And all the while the smell of fungus grew stronger as the damp grew damper.

In the light from the Grozzies' eyes, the tunnel revealed growths of strange fungus. It hung from the walls in slimy festoons or burst from crevices in flat shapes and explosive funnels, which leered out and seemed to suck you into their repulsive mouths. The further they went, the more the magpies saw the similarity between the fungus and the Grozzies. Sometimes the Grozzies seemed like walking versions of varieties they passed.

Later, they learned why they looked so alike. The reason was simple. The Grozzies had turned in on themselves. They'd become so cynical, so critical of anything living in the world above, they turned away from it even for food . . . except the creatures they captured, and they ate them out of sheer malice. So much had they come to depend on the underground fungus, they were growing more and more like it. They couldn't change, no more than malicious people in our part of the world seem able to change. And come to think of it, *they* begin to change slowly, too. Look at the face of someone who tittle-tattles and can never see any good in life. It becomes deformed and twisted, especially about the mouth.

So, it had come about that the Grozzies had realised almost too late they were changing into fungoids. Now they desperately wanted to return to the world above before the change was so complete and they were condemned to hang forever as slimy, sickening fungoids on the walls and floors of their own kingdom.

A few years before when all seemed hopeless and it looked certain their evil world at long last was about to turn in on itself forever, hope had come in the least likely form . . . an alley cat called (wait for it!) Mungo Brown. He was to be a send from whatever god the Grozzies had; though I suspect they were so inward-looking they had no god but themselves. Mungo was very like them in spirit so he became their god, expelled as he'd been from the world of light and beauty above because of the evil he'd done.

So there he was, that wicked alley cat, sat on a throne of black jade, awaiting the new prisoners the Grozzies were bringing back, Mungo the First, King of Grozzieland, crowned with a crown of red gold and many jewels. Smug in the royal chamber of Grozzieland he sat, oozing self-satisfaction and malicious glee as he watched the unfortunate magpies lugged in.

"Well, well, well," he purred, breathing on a jewelled ring before wiping it on his ermined gown. "Well, well, well," he purred again, grinning so broadly it seemed his very face would split. "What, or rather, who have we here? Two deserters from Wasteland all those years ago. Two of my best burglars who joined the other side . . . and had *me* put in that terrible gaol! Welcome to Grozzieland. I'm pleased to meet you once more."

Though they couldn't speak, the magpies heard every word, and *they* were far from pleased as you can imagine. They were also very astonished. Mungo gave another evil purr which lit him up more. The red light playing around him grew in intensity till he looked like a demon king in pantomime. He could never have acquired the dignity of a real king, he was such a low-bred cat, but he tried hard. Poor Mungo, he was always trying hard to be what he wasn't, and if he'd tried harder to be good, he might have become really great. Alas, he didn't put first things first. His priorities were all wrong, and if he'd put himself a little further down his list of priorities, he'd have gone far.

"Bring in our other guest," he ordered. "It's getting quite like old times."

Two Grozzies bowed low, then waddled out, returning shortly with Nero Squinks tucked unceremoniously under one arm and still grozzified.

"And now there are three," said Mungo, raising three jewelled fingers and leering at his captives round the dark glasses he wore. "One by one my enemies come to my kingdom . . . and how sweet is revenge! How pleased I am to have you three in my grasp!"

Mungo's voice thinned to a hiss, just like the Grozzies'. The hatred of many years were poured into his words. He walked round and round the grozzified trio hissing and snickering with glee, pinching them and telling the Grozzies what good meals they'd all make.

"Sooner or later . . . and I believe it will be sooner . . . the others will come looking for you," he went on. "Then, oh! what feasties we'll all have! Marinated magpie, roasted rat, braised hedgehog, vol-au-vent vole, onioned owl . . . and deep-fried, hotly fried, scalding hotly fried Fitzworthy! Oh, how I shall enjoy watching that aristocratic arch-enemy bake in his own kitchen. Watching him frizzle to the last whisker of burnt-up cat!"

As Mungo listed the dishes for his Grozzies, they began to hiss and drool. Their thick lips smacked alarmingly in sweet anticipation of the feasties in store. Some of them moved towards the magpies and rat, barely containing their hunger, but Mungo ordered them back with an impatient flick of his paw. Obedient as always, the Grozzies withdrew, bowing low before him, much to the trio's relief.

"Take 'em to the dungeons," said Mungo after another evil leer. "Let 'em wait there for the others to turn up. I wonder who'll next walk into my trap?"

Mack, Mick, and Nero were carried from the chamber, but before they went all three noticed how Mungo was becoming very much like a Grozzy himself. He walked heavily and talked lightly, hissing his sibilants like the creatures he ruled. Most of all, he gave off the same fungus smell which characterised that dismal kingdom. He was well on the way to becoming a feline fungoid.

Chapter 3

I suppose you're wondering how it was that Mungo came to be King of Grozzieland. You're not the only ones to be puzzled. Nero, Mick, and Mack were equally curious how Mungo became ruler of that dreadful place. They weren't long in finding out. True to his old self, Mungo couldn't resist visiting the dungeons to gloat, and when he gloated he talked too much. He told them the secret of his not being grozzified, why he was not affected by the Grozzies' deadly beams.

The secret lay in his dark glasses. He explained this and much else as he stood full of self-assurance and enjoying the misery of his three prisoners. "You see," he purred, chobbling a plateful of toadstools which evidently he'd grown fond of, for he ate the repulsive things constantly. "You see, when I was released from that frightful gaol in Wasteland, I was driven to the border and told to get out . . . never to show my face there again. They weren't particularly pleasant with me, but I'll get my own back before long, you'll see." He gave an angry flick of his tail, as if the memory of being chucked out of Wasteland still rankled. Then he continued, "I didn't waste my years in that squalid prison doing nothing, you know. I kept my head-piece ticking over smoothly . . . very smoothly. I planned my revenge every single day I spent in the wretched place.

Revenge entire and complete on *all* my enemies, starting with Horatio Fitzworthy and working down. I had a long list, and you three were high up on it!"

He stalked up and down the cell a while relishing his toadstools and thoughts of revenge. Both made him glow with satisfaction in more ways than one. "My first plan was to get power," he went on. "I can't live without power, and I had to get it at all costs. I was born to be great, you see, wasn't I?" Here he turned to his Grozzy guards, who bowed and grovelled, calling him all sorts of high-sounding titles like, "All Gracious Mungo!" and "Mungo the Supreme!" which pleased him no end.

"Quite right, quite right, my good people," he replied, handing round his plate of toadstool goodies. Then he turned back to his prisoners. "I studied hard and long, ready for the time I left gaol. You did me a good turn, Squinks, getting the prison library well stocked. I read everything I could lay my hands on and one day came across an old book about the Grozzies and their kingdom underground. I realised that if I could somehow overcome their rather off-putting habit of grozzifying, there was my way to power, my road to fame; for I saw that they needed me as much as I needed them."

Here he tapped his glasses. "These were the answer. Sunglasses. Polaroid. They cut out all danger rays including the Grozzy Alpha particles which are responsible for grozzification. I bought some pairs the day I was released and came down here. I also brought a lantern and a good supply of matches. My bright lantern frightened the hide off the first Grozzy I met, for they can't abide light at all. They fled from me all the way here, and once here I threatened 'em with electricity. And there you have it in a nutshell, or if you like . . . a light-bulb." He grinned at his own joke, but it fell flat on the others, the Grozzies included, who shivered at the mention of electricity.

*Grozzies bowing down before All Gracious Mungo
while chobbling toadstools*

"I subdued them in a twinkling, so to speak, and they crowned me king at once. They're not very bright, poor things, are you? But you trust me entirely." The Grozzies began grovelling again, fawning before him and trying to kiss his feet, but he kicked them away to avoid getting wet. "They're very willing, as you can see. They'd have served anyone who'd have got them out of the mess they've got themselves into. They know they'll turn into fungus if they stay here long enough, so they do anything I tell 'em because I've promised I'll get them out of this dismal place. They've helped enormously building my little gadgets down here. Soon we'll take over the world. The day isn't far off now." Mungo paused to breathe on his jewels and rub them on his gown to make them glitter. It was a habit he'd picked up since becoming king. He imagined all kings did it, and he wanted to do things right.

When he'd done, he looked up and said, "Just as I've discovered how to stop grozzification, so I've discovered how to put the sun and moon out of action. Two good shots with super-duper space-rockets and they'll be blown to bits." He lowered his voice for more effect. "I've built those rockets here. Once the sun and moon are out, the Grozzies can go safely to the world above . . . and there I'll be monarch, Emperor Mungo of Planet Earth!"

"Supreme, supreme!" hissed the Grozzies, falling down to worship him, and how he loved it! Mungo purred himself twice his size, and had they been able to peer behind those dark specs he wore, they'd have seen a faraway, dreamy look in his evil eyes. Having wallowed in their praises enough, he ordered the Grozzies out. He'd worked them to such a pitch, their minds ran along culinary lines again as they thought about the feasties up above and looked hungrily at Mick, Mack, and Nero. Some had even begun to pinch them to see how plump they were!

"I must send them away before they do you a mischief . . . and I want to be first doing that. You'll be quite safe till I give the word, though. Make yourselves comfortable meanwhile. I'll visit you again when your friends have arrived and once they're in the bag . . ." Here, Mungo rubbed his paws and left his sentence unfinished, but there was no doubt in his prisoners' minds what he meant. They were to be the bait to bring the others down to Grozzieland, and once their baiting days were done, their biting days started. Mungo made that quite clear as he turned the key in their cell and went off chuckling madly, "Oh, sweet revenge! Oh, sweet feasties for us all!" His insane voice trailed off as he went on his way, leaving his captives to the silence and the dark.

They said nothing for some hours till the effects of grozzification had worn off. Nero was the first to come to his senses. Having only one eye, he'd received only half the dosage of the other two. Not long after Mungo had gone, he felt tinglings and throbbings in his toes. The tingling spread upwards through the rest of his body as he slowly came back to life.

He rolled his one eye round its socket and blinked his eyelid twice when life returned to normal there. Then he murmured distantly, "Oh, dearie, dearie me!" He could think of nothing better to say for a while, so he said "Dearie me!" again several times before getting to his feet and walking to the magpies to examine them.

They sat still for another good hour, before there was a sad squawk from Mack, followed by a sadder one from Mick, who'd had his head bumped all the way down, for he'd been carried by a rather tall Grozzy.

"My, oh, my!" wailed Mack as he came to.

"Me, oh, me!" croaked Mick feeling the bumps on his head.

"How you two feeling?" asked Nero.

"Like nothing on earth," groaned Mack.

"I'm not surprised," commented Nero. "You're several thousand feet under it."

22

Mack ignored this and went on, "Did . . . did you hear what those terrible things said? What are we going to do? It's like some horrible nightmare. I can't believe it!"

"You'll have to, 'cos you're living it, not dreaming. And the quicker you believe it, the quicker we can sit down and think. I'll tell you what I've found out about this place while you're thinking," said Nero. "To begin with, don't ever touch any of those fungus things they eat."

"Why?" asked Mick.

"There's something very strange about them. Did you notice the glow Mungo gave off after he'd ate some?"

"You couldn't miss it," said Mack. "He lit up like an over-sized glow-worm."

"All Grozzies glow like that," observed Nero, who lowered his voice. "And it's my belief they're turning into toadstools just as Mungo said . . . and the fool can't see he's going the same way. Idiots like him are so full of their importance, they can never see when they're wrong."

"That could go for all of us," said Mack, giving the rat an old-fashioned look, for in their different ways the trio had gone very much off the rails during their lives.

Nero took the point. "It could, indeed," he said, "but some folk still remain bigger idiots than others. If Mungo would only open his eyes a little more, he'd see where he was going wrong. He'd notice there's peculiar stuff grows down here, and the deeper you go, the more peculiar it becomes."

"You ain't never been this deep before, have you, Nero?" asked Mack.

"Never," said the rat, "though I thought I'd explored every inch of the old workings. I'd heard about Grozzies, of course, but I never believed in 'em . . . till now. I always thought they were made-up stories."

"Some bloomin' story we're in now, mate," said Mack sadly. "I only hope it has a happy ending. Most fairy tales finish with a feast, but the way things is going, we're going to end up on the menu of this one!"

Nero didn't like that idea at all. He simply said, "We got to get out of here," and began feeling round the walls of their cell. The magpies joined him, casing the place from end to end, running their hands over every nick and cranny.

"Ugh!" said Mick, "It's lifting with creepy-crawlies!"

"And slippery-slimies!" added Mack, who'd withdrawn his hand rather quickly from a damp patch on the wall.

They came back to the middle of the cell and sat down.

"It's hopeless," said Mack sadly. "There ain't no way out nohow. I've cased it from end to end. There's only the door out . . . not even a window."

"Not much point putting a window in down here. There's nothing to look out at," observed Nero. "I only hope the others don't come searching for us. Old Mungo's using us as bait to catch them . . . and when he's got us all . . ." Here his voice trailed off. He didn't want to imagine what was going to happen to them then.

Mick, who wasn't the brightest of magpies, ventured, "Mungo said something about a party he was asking us to. Did he mean it?"

"Oh, yeah, he asked us to a party all right," Mack replied with disdain. "We'll be the life and soul of it. We'll be the grub!" It dawned on Mick what Mungo had meant, and he gave a soft moan. Mack continued, "I like parties, I do. No one better. But I was born to eat . . . not to be eaten!"

Further conversation stopped as they heard Grozzy guards slopping down the corridor. Their strange glow lit the cell through the bars in the door as they approached, but they were a long time coming. Their gait was slow and they were flat-footed. Like their dull light, they carried with them their own dull odour. They made the damp damper and the cold colder as they approached.

24

They halted outside and opened the hatch in the door. Mack saw the red eye of a Grozzy look through and immediately shut his eyes fast, but poor Mick gaped open-mouthed . . . and was grozzified for the next half-hour.

"Your suppersies," hissed a voice on the other side as something slid through the hatch. "Now be good boysies and eat it all up. We must keep ourselves plump and tender for the party."

The guard accompanying him slobbered in agreement. They heard him distinctly smacking his fat lips in a slow, drooly way. On the shelf of the hatch were three trays with food and three cups. There was also a lantern, suitably shaded, a little candle, and some safety matches.

"Now you must never light the candle or matches while we're about," warned the Grozzy guard. "If you're naughty and light up before we've gone, you'll be dreadfully punished. And none of us want that, do we? We all want to remain such good friendsies for the feastie and make it a happy, happy party." They thought he added something like "Yum, yum!" but they weren't sure. Then the guards pushed off.

As the light from the Grozzies grew dim, Mack lit the candle. He was about to take a swig from his mug when Nero stopped him. The rat sniffed his drink, sniffed the food, and said, "The drink's all right. It smells like some sort of tea, but leave the food alone. It's made from fungus. Some kind of pizza they're fond of down here. They're wanting to fatten us up to suit their own palates. We'll just have to eat bread and drink tea from now on."

Mack looked gloomily at the plate before him. The meal certainly looked very tasty and he was particularly fond of pizzas . . . of any food! "Are you sure we'll turn into blooming toadstools or something if we eat this?" he asked.

"You'll turn into something more horrible. You'll become more edible, that's for sure, if you touch it," Nero replied. "You'll become even more attractive on the Grozzies' menu."

Mack moaned. He *did* love his food, but though he liked it, he'd no desire to change places with it. "Well, I ain't going to be nobody's mushroom soup," he said. "They eat me as I am, or not at all. Preferably the latter!" And he picked up his dry crust and ate slowly.

They noticed Mick wasn't eating. Nero turned, asking why he didn't take his tray and eat. He looked closer and waved his paw before Mick's face. He was zonked out.

"The idiot must have looked at the Grozzy guard. And after all we've said!" exclaimed his partner. "Serve him right if we eats his supper for him. My, oh, my! Will Mick never learn!"

The candlelight allowed them to explore the cell more closely. It wasn't anything like the nice, cosy cells in the Black Wood police station. It was cold, forbidding, and miserable. Trickles of slime ran down walls, and horrible crawly things slid slowly from one nook to the other. Festoons of fungus hung everywhere, and from the cracks between the paving stones, clusters of toadstools popped up. Clearly the cell had been used for many years, because age-old dates were scrawled on the walls with faded names and initials.

Near a pair of rusty manacles was an ominous set of scratch-marks, as if some poor prisoner had tried to claw his way out in desperation. The one means of exit was by the door; a great, metal door hanging on great, rusty hinges punctured by an even rustier keyhole. In the door were two hatches; one for passing in food, and the other, smaller and higher, for peering in at the prisoners. It was through this Mick was grozzified.

While Mack went one way round the cell, Nero went the other. In the end, after they'd met in the middle, Mack observed sadly, "There ain't a single blooming way out at all."

"Unless we try the floor," suggested Nero, ever the optimist.

"Not a hope," said Mack, who'd tested every flagstone to see if it was hollow underneath. "They're set in solid earth. If we did go down, we'd only go deeper . . . an' I don't want to go deeper here, thank you very much!"

They sat next to Mick, who was still staring into space. Both of them thunk hard, and after a while Mack said, "I suppose all we can do now is wait . . . wait for something or someone to turn up." He let out a huge sigh and Nero blew out the candle to save it. It made the darkness which had dropped on their lives darker. They were cold, hungry, and without hope; but had they known it, help was already on its way. It was to come from the least likely of sources . . . one could say the smallest: from young Pip Fieldmouse, the cadet who'd been left in charge of Black Wood police station and whom we left happily drinking fizzy lemonade.

Chapter 4

A quality which Pip Fieldmouse had plenty of was enterprise. He'd been a bright lad at school and come out on top, mainly through hard work and enterprise. And if any of you don't know what enterprise is, it's seeing a problem, weighing it up, and tackling it straight away with no messing about. He was also very determined to get on in life, for his mother, a poor widow, had sacrificed much to give him a good education at old Dorey's school in Meadowville.

So, when several days had passed and there was no sign of Mick and Mack, he knew he had a problem on his hands. He decided at once to go and see what had happened. But first, being the diligent police-cadet he was, he watered the flowers in the front cell and was about to leave the station key with Mrs. Flit across the road, when he remembered what Mack had said about the mushrooms. He popped into the back cell and it was a good job he did. There was a magnificent crop of button mushrooms that morning, the finest champignons they'd had all summer.

"I'd better pick these and take them along with me. Nero Squinks likes mushrooms, I know," he said. "Otherwise they'll have gone off by the time I get back."

So he picked and picked till the rush basket was full. Then, covering them with damp paper, he locked up the station and went across to Mrs. Flit's shop.

He explained at some length why he was setting out and where he was going, but the longer he spoke, the more Mrs. Flit looked worried. At length, when he'd done, she said, "Young man, I think you ought to inform someone else apart from me. This looks very serious. I mean, anything could have happened. I wouldn't know what to do if *you* don't come back! What would an old woman like me do with a police station on her hands?"

Police-cadet Fieldmouse raised his cap and scratched the back of his furry head. It hadn't crossed his mind that he might not come back. He was so full of self-confidence ... but I must admit, so inexperienced ... that events like not coming back hadn't happened in his young life before. He found the prospect rather disturbing.

"I-er-I suppose you have a point there, Mrs. Flit," he said, looking worried for a moment. Then his face brightened. "However, just to make sure, perhaps you wouldn't mind sending word with Bert Squirrel, the carrier, when he goes to Hedgehog Meadow today. Ask him to call on Quill Hedgehog, please, and let him know what's happened. Sergeant Mack said I was always to tell Quill if I ran into any trouble while he and Mick were away."

Having taken this decision, he felt much better, picked up his basket and wished Mrs. Flit good-day. He marched confidently into the street, whistling a happy tune and greeting folk he passed. Mrs. Flit took off her apron as soon as he'd gone, put on her coat and bonnet, and hurried to Bert Squirrel before he started the daily trip to the Meadow Shire.

An hour or so's steady walking brought Pip to the entrance of the old mineshaft under the Mystery Marshes. He approached it cautiously and peered in. It looked black, very black ... scarifyingly black! His little whiskers twitched ten to the dozen and his eyes flicked nervously all round that black hole. Then he put one foot inside.

A large, black thing flapped noisily out of the tunnel squawking like mad. It made him jump. He stood stock still, but nothing happened. This time he poked his nose further inside, sniffing the air for scent, peering till his eyes ached.

He heard and saw nothing, but he did smell something ... a strange, fungoid smell. At first, he thought it came from his basket of mushrooms, but the further he went into the tunnel, the stronger the scent became. It wasn't mushrooms, for they smelled fresh and clean. It was something else he didn't recognise but felt he knew. The more he advanced, the smaller he seemed to become for he was very scared, though he'd never have admitted it. He was a tiny fieldmouse, the tiniest of a small family of fieldmice; yet it was his small size—and his basket of mushrooms—which saved the day.

He'd gone a long, long way down the mineshaft when he came to the place where the Grozzies had broken through. Fortunately for Pip, he'd very keen hearing, so that when he heard strange, slurping noises drift up the tunnel, and as the very first glimmerings of Grozzy light appeared, he put out his light.

Nearer and nearer came the slow, sloshy steps of a Grozzy patrol. Brighter and brighter grew the light they gave out, and so close were they approaching that Pip made out two separate beams moving this way and that. He was lucky those beams didn't fall directly on him else he'd have been grozzified—and there'd have been a very different ending to this story.

He had the sense to realise that if he panicked and ran back the way he'd come, they'd hear him. But what was worse, he very quickly realised he couldn't retreat. The same wet footfalls were also coming down the opposite direction, the way he'd come. He was trapped!

He was a very frightened fieldmouse, I can tell you, but his nerve didn't fail. His schooling had been of the best. As he looked wildly round for some means of escape, he noticed a ledge, a very small ledge near the roof of the tunnel. It was so small, in fact, it was where workmen put their lunch-boxes for safe-keeping in the olden days. Without more ado he scrambled up the side of the tunnel, leaving his basket of mushrooms on the floor.

Slosh, slosh, slurp, slurp, came the two Grozzy patrols towards each other. Pip drew himself back as far as he could to make himself unseen. Tiny as he was, he dearly wished then he might have been tinier. In fact, he wished he wasn't there at all! He heard them call out as they approached and their hissy, scratchy voices sent shivers down his back.

"There's somebody here. I heard him distinctly," hissed a Grozzy.

"Hello there!" called back another voice from the opposite direction. "It's us! We heard something, too. Whoever it was hasn't passed us."

At this point Pip peeped over the rim of his ledge. His eyes grew wide with astonishment. He was looking at real Grozzies. They were exactly as old Codger Squeak had described them scores of times and he'd never believed him. Leastways, not when he'd grown up. Yet there they were before his very eyes . . . Grozzies in all their gruesome grozziness. Their lights began to search all about the tunnel and Pip remembered old Squeak's warning. "If you see 'em, don't look into their eyes," he'd said. "They'll knock you senseless as soon as they look at you."

Pip drew back. Their lights searched and searched, but none of them suspected that on a ledge scarcely a foot above them cowered a tiny fieldmouse hardly believing what he heard and saw.

When they'd met up, the patrols began to identify each other, as Mungo had taught them. He was very keen no one should ever get into Grozzieland unseen, and his patrols were out all the time. "Who are you?" shouted the leader of one patrol. "Call out your namesies and be identified!"

"Daedalia Quercina," came the reply from a Grozzy who suffered from an advanced state of woodrot.

"Poria Monticola," hissed his partner, who also suffered from the same malady. They were a very spongy couple.

Poria Monticola then challenged the other patrol. He had a sort of brown, crumbly face, a face which looked as though it was falling apart, and it terrified Pip when he saw him. "Stand forth and be identified!" he called out very officiously. Of course, they all knew who they were, but not being very bright they went through this rigmarole every time, as Mungo had instructed. They were, to tell the truth, scared stiff of him.

"Captain Coniophora Cerebella and Merulius Lacrymans!" spat back a very pompous Grozzy. He had a puffy, purple face and was full of his own grozziness. His companion was quite different, a wispy sort of person who looked always on the point of lapsing into complete wetness like soaked cotton-wool.

"I could have sworn I heard someone," said the captain. Then his eye caught the mushrooms. "Why!" he exclaimed, "What have we here?"

The quartet of Grozzies gathered over the basket and hissed together, "Mushroomsies!"

Then began an elbowing and shoving which was quite unseemly. I've seen some school-dinner queues in my time, some quite unruly ones, but the pushing and grabbing of the Grozzies beat anything I've laid eyes on. And their eating habits . . . why, they were quite repulsive! They grabbled and grobbled, slurped and burped as they polished off the huge basket of mushrooms in one minute, twenty seconds flat.

As they chobbled away, Pip also noticed another strange thing. As the mushrooms went in, so more of their light came out. The more mushroomy they themselves became; and when they'd polished them off, they slumped down, holding full tummies and hissing softly as the mushrooms took effect.

It was some time before they spoke again, but when they did, Pip learned some very useful information.

Poria Monticola was the first to surface, "Whoever is in here, is still in. He hasn't got past us," he said.

"Then he must have gone down deeper, to Grozzieland through one of the side-shafts," said Captain Coniophora, pointing to the way he'd come. "Let's get after him before he finds out there's a rocket-launching base. He'll pass it on the way down. If King Mungo finds out, we'll all be in trouble, and if the rocketsies aren't fired, we'll never have earth mushroomsies like these again."

"Whoever he is, he grows scrumptious mushroomsies. He'd taste nice fried with his own mushroomsies," commented Monticola slurpily.

At this, Pip shivered so mightly he almost fell off the ledge. It was fortunate the Grozzies moved away for he couldn't control his quaking at all after Monticola's comment. He listened till their footsteps could be heard no more, then he scrambled from the ledge and was off . . . back up the tunnel as fast as his legs could carry him.

Once outside, he moved faster. Indeed, he ran so hard he caught up with Bert Squirrel's old horse as it set out for Meadow Shire, a full hour late.

"Stop! Stop!" he yelled, rushing up to the aged carrier and horse.

Police-cadet Pip drops in on Bert Squirrel's horse

"What's the matter, young Pip?" asked the squirrel with the slow drawl of his kind.

"Everything," gasped the fieldmouse. "I've simply got to get to Hedgehog Meadow as quickly as possible. Please make your horse go faster," he concluded, jumping alongside the old carrier.

"Oh, I don't know about that," drawled the squirrel, scratching his head. "My owd horse ain't never gone fast in his whole life. We don't move quick down our way. I don't s'pose he knows how to move quick, not at his time o' life. There ain't never been no 'casion to move quick afore . . . no, not ever. 'Taint no good starting now, young Pip."

The ancient animal had an old, straw hat on its head through which its ears poked. Those ears were pricked as the carter spoke. It was almost as if the nag knew what was being said. It went slower and slower till it halted under a large chestnut tree. And there it stayed. Nothing would coax it into the hot sunshine again. It closed its eyes, hung its lip, and settled down for a long nap.

Furious, Pip shouted and bellowed. Even Bert Squirrel tried a few homely clucks, but the horse wouldn't budge. Pip stopped shouting. He was about to get off and walk when he had a bright idea. He was chock full of 'em. He glanced at the branches over the horse, thinking about the times his mother had been surprised by uninvited guests dropping in. He'd noticed how on such occasions his mother sprang suddenly to life, rushing about here and there tidying things up. If only he could "drop in" on the horse, he thought, perhaps it would move.

With great speed he shinnied up the tree and crawled along the branch directly over the horse. It stood snoring, blissfully unaware it was about to be dropped in on. Its ears flicked away the flies as it dreamed of green pastures and long, lingering days of summer.

Then, with a yell like a battle cry, Pip let go and dropped in!

Never was a horse more shocked. It looked up and its eyes rolled wildly. At Pip's cry, the pastures green turned bloody with battle. The horse dreamed of war and carrying knights into the fray. The years rolled off its back as young Pip landed, and it was changed in the twinkling of an eye!

If it had grown wings and taken off like Pegasus, a more astonishing change could not have taken place. It rolled its eyes again, opened its nostrils wide, blew out a hot snort, and began pawing the earth, as if winding itself up like a great spring. Then it neighed a neigh like thunder that shook the surrounding countryside. Frightened birds and animals took off in all directions . . . and so did the horse.

The spring unwound. It reared on its hind-legs, then bounded off, Pip, carter, and cart loosed in a cloud of dust from which they shot like an arrow. Pip hung on like grim death. So did Bert Squirrel, his mouth still hanging wide from surprise. Away went the horse's hat, the driver's cap and whip. Away went his reins and half his load before the horse stopped.

It raced down the road to the Meadow Shire, eating the miles and scattering all before it. Farmers were left trying to control their own plunging steeds, fired by the horse which passed. The whole countryside was left in turmoil. Hens scattered in the hamlets they raced through and never laid again. Cats shot from sleepy windowsills and were lost forever. Dogs went yelping for cover, and ancient roadmen fled their work and dived into hedgerows as the horse approached, bursting their barricades and leaving all chaos. The Black Wood and Meadow Shire had seen nothing like it and, mercifully, never did again.

The brute stopped as suddenly as it started, digging its hooves into the green turf of Hedgehog Meadow. Cart and carter came to an abrupt halt, Pip to an abrupter one. He went flying over the horse's head to be joined a second later by Bert. Thump! Thump! They landed alongside each other and tried to recover their wits.

And the horse? After two or three ungracious snorts and another great neigh, he settled down. His old expression fell on his face and he stood looking sleepily at the pair on the earth as if nothing had happened. His dream was done. It had faded and gone. He never galloped after.

All Bert could say was, "Well, I never!" over and over, scratching his head as if he didn't believe it. All Pip said was, "Well, I did!" and thanked the perplexed driver, who had all sorts of explaining to do on the way back. Then Pip walked quickly to Quill's house at the Great Oak Tree on the other side of the Meadow.

Chapter 5

Quill was in his garden. He was busy hoeing the onions and weeding leeks, which grew greenly in a very green corner of his vegetable plot. Flowering runner-beans scrambled up tripods, converting them to green tepees splashed scarlet. The last broad-bean flowers hung heavy with scent and wooed tireless bees from the nearby wood. Long rows of purple potato flowers glistened in the sun, sucking its light to the white spuds swelling beneath. But what caught Pip's attention as he entered the place were the succulent strawberries nestling under their canopy of netting which kept the thieving birds away.

Quill looked up as the gate clicked open. He was surprised to see young Pip, more surprised to see his bedraggled state for he hadn't had time to straighten himself up.

"Bless me!" said the hedgehog. "What's been happening to you, young man?"

Pip told him, then he told him more; told him about the Grozzies. Quill could hardly believe his ears, and when the fieldmouse had done, Quill wasn't simply holding his hoe, he was leaning on it for support. "Grozzies!" he exclaimed. "Grozzieland . . . King Mungo Brown . . . Nero, Mick, and Mack taken prisoners? It doesn't seem real. But then, neither did my other adventures at the time.

Well, well, well, so mad Mungo's turned up again. I half-expected it. His sort never disappear."

Pip had begun brushing himself down, so the hedgehog invited him into the house. "We must get some help, and that help can come only from the Great Beyond. You'll see how they do it when you get there. Combined brainpower it's called, based on the theory that more heads are better than one. But let's do first things first. I suppose you haven't eaten since you left the Black Wood Shire?"

Pip murmured something about not having time. Everything had been such a rush, but he followed the kindly hedgehog into his kitchen. The inside of the Great Oak Tree was Quill's cottage. Its cool, brick floor and whitened walls were refreshing after the heat outside. The cuckoo clock fluted two as they went in . . . then popped out again silently to have another look at Pip. The old grandfather clock in the corner grumbled inwardly, then also coughed up two, before retiring for half-an-hour's snooze.

They walked into the dining room where the table was set for tea. Having sent Pip upstairs to wash, Quill returned to the kitchen for another set of eating irons. He also brought back some sandwiches, lettuce, tomato, and cucumber, with a few radishes and spring onions straight from his garden. He put a little pot on the table containing celery, so that when the fieldmouse came back, he needed no second invitation to tuck in. Between sandwich bites and celery nibbles he told Quill the whole story.

When he'd done, Quill said again, "Bless me!" and chewed thoughtfully on a particularly long stick of celery he'd laced with salt. At length he spoke. "Of course, I've heard of Grozzies before. Who hasn't? But I never really believed they existed. The Mystery Marsh folk are full of such tales . . . and we've all sorts of stories here in the Meadow about witches and elves and all that . . . but Grozzies! Well, I never. Bless me!"

*Pip finds Quill hoeing and weeding his garden
in Hedgehog Meadow*

Quill felt so amazed that he had to bring himself round by suggesting they had strawberries. Pip endorsed his suggestion. He thought it was excellent. He thought it even better . . . if you can get anything better than 'excellent' . . . when Quill brought in a large jug of cream and a sugar-sprinkler to go with them. At the sight of the blue-ringed jug and mound of strawberries peeping over the rim of the bowl, the cadet's mouth began to water.

It positively drooled as the hedgehog ladled strawberries into the dishes he'd brought. Pip watched every move, his eyes sliding back and forth in time with Quill's arm. Then, having filled their dishes, he lifted the jug and a torrent of delicious cream spilled over the fruit. The fieldmouse gasped and held onto his chair to stop his fingers grabbing his spoon and digging in.

Quill finished decorating his own well-filled dish with the cream jug, then said, "Do start up, young fellow." Pip did!

And what strawberries they were! Quill was renowned for them. "Succulent" or "delicious" had no meaning when describing those strawberries. A new word, a whole new language was needed. They were "scrumchuculous," "exchoculatingly scrumchuculous!" They melted in your mouth and filled your whole being with delight. In homage to Quill's strawberries they ate in silence till the bowl was empty and the jug quite dry.

Full to his eyebrows, young Pip thanked Quill from the bottom of his heart. "Don't mention it," said the hedgehog. "I'm glad you enjoyed it, and it'll have to last for we've a longish trip ahead to the Great Beyond."

The fieldmouse looked abashed. "Please, Mr. Quill," he said, "I haven't brought my toothbrush or anything . . ."

"Not to worry, not to worry," said Quill kindly. "I've plenty spare of everything in my guest-room. We'll have you sorted out in no time. Now take this," and he handed the cadet a large, tartan hold-all, which he began filling from a variety of cupboards and drawers. When it was full, he passed the fieldmouse a flying helmet and a pair of goggles, with a long scarf to wrap round his neck.

"What's these for?" asked Pip.

"For flying, that's what they're for," replied Quill in a matter-of-fact way. He was quite used to it by now. As in our world, Humanland, things have moved rapidly in the Animalfolk world over the past few years. "We're going in the flying-machine Hoot Owl made for me. How else do you think we can get quickly to the Great Beyond? It would take days on foot. With my flying-machine, I can pop over just when I want. Now then, young squeaker, get a move on. I'll lock up and my housekeeper, Mrs. Blossom, will clear away when she comes to clean tomorrow. I'll scribble her a note telling her where we're going."

Quill picked up the stub of a pencil and wrote Mrs. Blossom a short note. She came three times a week to do his cleaning, and she looked after his house when he went on his travels. He put the note by the cuckoo clock, then locked his door securely, hiding the key in the secret place only he and Mrs. Blossom knew about.

Then he led Pip to the big shed in the field behind his house. It hadn't been built very long and Pip was curious about it, wondering what was in there. He was soon to find out. Quill flung open the doors . . . and there stood the flying-machine, gleaming and ready to go.

It was not unlike the one the Great Beyonders used in their Wasteland adventure, but it was smaller and more compact. It held only the pilot and a passenger. Pip had to stow his luggage under his feet, but it was a delightful machine despite the lack of space; the sort of thing you can invent by doodling, with all manner of fascinating gadgets in it. It was a masterpiece of Hootavention.

Although it looked like a Humanfolk plane, it was very different. It ran on the natural system. Animalfolk are very adept at turning natural things to use. They're much more conservation-minded than us, for we can be very wasteful at times.

To begin with, the flying-machine didn't need fuel. It relied on the energy of the pilot and his passenger to keep it airborne, though it could run on solar energy on long trips. All the pilot and passenger had to do was pedal to keep it going . . . and to pedal in a very leisurely way once it was in the air. They didn't have to groan and puff as I do when I cycle any distance. By an ingenious system of gears and levers, it was possible to get it off the ground, then the rest was easy. Once up, you switched to solar energy or a natural fuel Hoot had discovered in trees called arborol.

Quill released the plane from its brakes and went to the port-side wing. "Now, young Pip, if you go to the other wing and help me push her out, we'll be ready in a jiffy," he said.

The fieldmouse went to the starboard wing, and though he had to reach high and stand tip-toe to push, the machine rolled effortlessly onto the green runway, kept mowed and rolled by Quill specially for the flying-machine, the Hootaplane Mark I.

Pip gazed in awe. He'd never seen such a machine in all his life; at least, not close. Occasionally he'd seen one floating through the sky over Black Wood Shire, but he'd never been close enough to actually touch one, let alone fly in an aeroplane. The prospect quite took his breath away.

Quill pointed to the rear seat. "Now climb aboard, my lad," he said. "And when I tell you, pedal for all you're worth. With two of us on board and all our luggage, it's going to take a bit more effort to get us off the ground."

Pip climbed in, peering over the cockpit at Quill who was getting into the pilot's seat. "Supposing we don't make it," he ventured.

"Then we land up in the hedge at the bottom of the Meadow. But don't worry. It's never happened yet . . . and they say the hedge is quite comfortable, those who live down there. Now fasten your seat-belt and start pedalling when I tell you."

The hedgehog took the controls and adjusted several switches and knobs. Then he turned and gave the field-mouse the thumbs-up sign. Pip started pedalling like mad. At first, he glanced over the side, but the sight of the ground whizzing by was too much for him. He closed his eyes. He daren't for the life of him look at the great hedge looming nearer and nearer each second.

Slowly the propellers began turning; then, as they gathered speed, they whirled faster, rolling down the slope towards the hedge at the bottom. Just when it seemed they wouldn't make it and go hurtling into the mass of beech leaves, the plane gave two or three little bumps, a gentle shudder . . . and she was up!

The propellers whizzed faster, and when Quill pulled on the joystick, the aircraft climbed steeply. The air sang in Pip's ears. He felt it rush past his face tearing at the scarf which streamed behind him. Inside his goggles he opened one eye, then the other. He looked down as if drawn by magnets, just in time to see the hedge go skimming by a foot or two beneath them. It made his tummy heave, but he gulped with relief. When he looked up, all that he saw was a long stretch of blue sky and some wispy clouds floating lazily over Hedgehog Meadow.

Below, the land was a patchwork of fields and copses, long, green meadows, and golden cornfields. Cows stopped their endless chewing to look up. They stared dully a while, after the way of cows, then resumed their browsing. In the next field, a young colt took fright, cantering round and round his paddock. He'd never seen an aircraft before. Labourers in the fields straightened their backs, putting gnarled hands to shade their eyes as they squinted at the speck high above. Children waved their handkerchiefs, and Quill dipped his wings in reply. He always did this when he went to the Great Beyond.

In time, the Staying Hills rose before them. The going was much easier than Pip imagined. In fact, it was almost restful pedalling away slowly and without effort, scooping the air as a swimmer lazily pulls water past when enjoying a dip.

"You all right back there?" asked Quill over his shoulder.

"Yes, sir. It's great!" came back the excited reply.

"Good," said the hedgehog. "Another hour or so and we'll be at Horatio's place, Fitzworthy Castle. I hope he's in and not on his travels."

Pip had heard much about Horatio from Sergeant Mack, so he knew the cat lived in a castle built long ago, a castle which was home, too, to any friends who called to see him. He'd longed for years to see it. Now he was on his way there.

They had to pedal faster to clear the Staying Hills and the cloud on top. For some time Pip saw nothing but clammy mist. It seemed eerie plunging into it from the bright sunshine, but when they emerged, they were clear of the hills and high above the plain below. Pip saw the Great Beyond unroll before him like a map, stretching to the haze of the far horizon.

A river started somewhere in the hills and raced in glistening torrents to the plain. There it decided it had had enough of hurry and bustle. It slowed and widened, moving lazily in long meanders across the land.

Harvest had already started. Field after field was shorn and crisp, yellow stubble flung back its brightness where shortly before slender corn had waved. Heavy carts laden with sheaves still trundled back and forth to bursting barns and stacks. In the fields, labourers toiled to gather the last of the crop before the weather broke.

Dotted here and there were red-tiled hamlets and farms. Dew-ponds winked and streams gleamed. Once, a stiff-armed windmill, white and erect, turned its sails in salute and a whey-faced miller rubbing his hands on his apron came to the door to wave. The whole land smiled with the fulsomeness that only harvest-time brings. It was a long, long way from Grozzieland and the dismal depths where Mungo and his sad minions lived, plotting to blot out the sun.

Fitzworthy Castle stood in a meander of the river, which formed a natural moat. Just over the moat lay the castle's gardens, formally laid out and immaculately kept. Rows of topiarised yews stood guard over neighbouring flower-beds that led to the great drawbridge, now permanently lowered. Sheltered by a walled garden near the castle was a healthy vegetable plot.

Not far away was a cricket-field, for the Great Beyonders were keen sportsmen. They played for the fun of it, and that day happened to be the annual match between Horatio's team and Brushy Fox's eleven from the Wood and Riverbank. Quill and Pip saw the ground and the players, ranged like white chessmen, on the pitch. The hedgehog circled the ground twice before he came in, landing his plane neatly on the recreation field next to the cricket-pitch. Brushy Fox's side were batting, and Brushy greeted them as they clambered from the aircraft.

"My dear, old chappie," said the fox, grasping the hedgehog's paw and shaking it warmly. "How delighted I am to see you! You've dropped in exactly at the right time. We Woodlanders are about to drub Horatio's lot for the first time since I don't know when. Old Bill Badger is hammering them something wicked."

Plucking off their flying-helmets and goggles, they followed Brushy to the marquee. Over it hung three little flags of the Fitzworthy Cricket Club, on each of the main poles. It was cool inside where trestle-tables and chairs were set. Inside, Quill met more old friends who'd shared in his adventures in the past. Rachel Water-Rat, Olive Otter, and Vicky Vole were tidying up the remnants of the meal the cricketers had enjoyed during the interval.

"Why, if it isn't dear, old Quill!" exclaimed Olive, rushing over and giving the hedgehog a great hug—prickles and all! She wasn't the only one delighted to see him, for Rachel and Vicky, hearing the other greet their friend, came from the kitchen and each in turn hugged him as close as the otter had done. Pip stood by amazed. He didn't realise just how many friends the hedgehog had. Folk were coming up and greeting him on all sides.

The Animalfolk girls quickly rustled him some grub, then turned their attention—or perhaps I should say "affection"—on little Pip, when Quill introduced him. Now they mothered and petted him, offering all the goodies they had in the tent, till he was almost bursting with fizzy lemonade, ice-cream, and cream cakes! He was rescued by Brushy, who led out the two animals to watch the final stages of the match, seating them on comfortable deck chairs to witness the last over.

Horatio was bowling and the badger faced him, his huge shoulders crouched over the bat and his eyes fixed on Horatio, who came loping in at a cracking pace. The ball fell short and crack! Bill's shoulders opened and the little sphere of red leather soared high, joining the swallows near the square-leg boundary.

"Tu-woo!" said Hoot Owl, the umpire, watching the ball disappear over the pavilion. "What a hit!" and he raised both wings to signal a six. The Woodlanders and Riverbankers cheered madly. They'd won, and their supporters stood to clap the teams in.

"Good show, you chaps," said Brushy Fox, clapping his hand on the badger's shoulder and Frisk Otter, who'd been his partner. "You did well. What a splendid game it's been!" He went to Horatio and thanked him for the match, tell-

Horatio bowls and Big Bill Badger faces him
at Fitzworthy Cricket Club

ing him they hoped to do the same at River Meadow the next year where they had their own pitch. Horatio laughed goodheartedly and shook the fox's hand.

"Getting a bit long in the tooth these days for this sort of thing. Time I stood down to let some of you young Animalfolk take over," he said, winking at Vicky Vole who was dishing out more iced lemonade to the thirsty players, along with Old Mole.

"Nonsense," she replied. "You're good for the next twenty seasons."

The cat smiled amiably and motioned them to the tent. They were hot and ready for the lemonade Old Mole, his butler, was serving from a jug; and great was Horatio's surprise when he saw Quill.

"Well, if it isn't Quill!" he exclaimed, grasping the hedgehog's paw and pumping it like mad. "This is a surprise . . . and a very pleasant one, too!" As he spoke, he slipped on his blazer and munched a sandwich. He glanced keenly at Quill for he guessed some emergency had brought him to the Great Beyond. When he came on a regular visit, he always let them know in good time. But Animalfolk never speak directly about their problems when they first meet. They let them drift quietly into the conversation at the right time. Horatio politely waited for the right time.

When he'd finished his drink, Quill handed his glass to Old Mole and drew Horatio to one side. "I didn't like to say anything at once," he began, "but when you've a moment, I've something rather urgent to discuss. Trouble, real trouble has sprung up in Domusland. In fact, Mungo has sprung up again . . . or rather he's gone down, under the Mystery Marshes, where Mick and Mack with Nero Squinks have disappeared. If you put two and two together . . ."

"As usual they add up to Mungo Brown's having something to do with the answer," concluded Horatio.

"Exactly," said Quill.

The cat paused in the middle of nibbling his sandwich. For a moment, and only for a moment, something like anger appeared in his eyes, for he was the most mild-tempered of cats. Then he finished eating and said quietly, "Perhaps it might be better to discuss this at my place. That wretched alley cat still has friends here, believe it or not . . . strange folk who think like him and want to turn our beautiful land into . . . well, to what it was when he had control. Some folks will do anything for money and power. I'll get the others back to the castle where we can talk in peace. We always gather there anyhow after a match."

Full to his furry ears, Pip had been keeping in the background. He was quite overwhelmed at actually seeing all those famous people Mick and Mack had spoken of so often. Noticing him by himself, Olive Otter took the little fieldmouse over to where Quill was speaking with Horatio; then she went back to help her friends tidy up.

"Meet a young friend of mine from Black Wood Shire," said Quill. "It's his alertness and courage that's brought us here today. We'd have known nothing of what Mungo's up to till it was too late, if Pip hadn't kept his head. Meet Police-cadet Pip Fieldmouse, Horatio. He's a real credit to the force." The fieldmouse would have crept away if he could, but Horatio was already shaking his paw and saying how pleased he was to have him with them. "I'm very pleased to make your acquaintance, young man," he said.

Pip saluted smartly and said the pleasure was entirely his. Then he retired behind Quill once more. The cat suggested they all go to his castle without further ado to hear what Pip had to say, and he led the way, with a wide-eyed fieldmouse keeping close to Quill.

Chapter 6

The sun was setting as the animals trooped across the drawbridge, and the castle walls were softened by its light. Many years of history had mellowed those walls, now covered with delicate lichen. On the highest turret, the flag of the Great Beyond fluttered in the merest hint of breeze, and added to the serenity the whole land enjoyed . . . quite different from when President Mungo Brown had control.

As we've noted, the drawbridge was rarely raised; indeed, so rarely that grass had started growing between the planks and where the bridge rested on the land. The planks were thick and sturdy so that the footsteps of those crossing could scarcely be heard. In the old days, when the Wastelanders had occupied the castle and made it their headquarters, the drawbridge would have been raised about this time. But now it stayed firmly down, a welcome for all guests who came to the castle . . . and many there were throughout the year.

Passing through what had been a guardroom, now a lodge, they entered the courtyard with its ancient well, the very well Hoot Owl had led the raid through years before, when Frisk and the others had been rescued. Now, all was peaceful. Where the Wasteland rats had paraded and drilled, a large rose garden bloomed. Round it sanded walks skirted the flower beds. The breeze didn't reach here, so the heavy scent of roses hung everywhere.

"Delightful!" said Brushy, sniffing a particularly beautiful rose. "What d'you call this?" Brushy, too, was a keen rose-grower.

"We call it 'Felinus's Fancy' in memory of my father. He loved roses. We named this new variety after him. It won first prize in the village show last week. A great one for roses was Father Felinus."

Other roses sprayed scent about them, flinging their colours with rash abandon. A walk through Horatio's courtyard was a walk through Paradise and the animals knew it, continuing in silence till they'd reached the library indoors.

Now the library was a wonderful place like all good libraries. Thick, leather-bound volumes reached high above them, shelf on shelf, to the ceiling. The room was oak-panelled, rich with waxed furniture and oiled books. In the middle stood a large table ringed by wooden chairs, whose legs were as ornately carved as the table itself. Horatio's desk was nearer the French windows at one end of the room, opposite an open fireplace with the Fitzworthy Arms carved on a stone tablet above.

Oil paintings of Fitzworthys stretching back into the past hung in recesses, jumping to life when the candelabra over the table was lit. Like a graceful ballerina, it hung suspended from the ceiling dripping glass. As they went in Horatio switched it on. Light danced everywhere from the pendants, showering on the table, making the old paintings gleam as they warmed to life.

Pip gazed open-mouthed. He was even more overcome with shyness at all this splendour, particularly as they put him in the place of honour next to Horatio at the head of the table. He was so tiny an extra cushion had to be brought to raise him up.

52

Around sat the Great Beyonders, mootmen all of them, elected elders of their various witans throughout the shires in the Great Beyond. Stalwart honest Animalfolk each one. Going clockwise round the table were: Horatio and Pip, then Quill and Brushy, Big Bill Badger, Frisk Otter, Olive, his sister, stocky Spade Mole, Rachel Water-Rat, Vicky Vole, and her cousin Pippa, more otters, then Hoot Owl, who sat the other side of Horatio. Pip sank as far as he could in the plump cushion, barely able to raise his eyes over the table to look at the others whose eyes were fixed on him.

When they'd settled down to a cup of tea Old Mole, the butler, brought, Horatio knocked on the table and asked for silence. "Friends," he began, "Quill has brought us urgent news . . . sad news, I'm afraid. If I mention the name of Mungo Brown you'll guess at once how urgent it is . . . and how sad it must be."

A buzz of conversation ran round the table at Mungo's name. Hoot uttered a quick "Tu-woo!" and Bill Badger gave a low growl. The cat continued, "It appears, my friends, that our old enemy has reappeared . . . surfaced would hardly be the right word . . . in or under the Mystery Marshes. This very courageous police-cadet, Pip Fieldmouse, actually went there, risking his own safety, to locate some . . . what did you call them?"

"Grozzies, sir," said Pip, looking up quickly, then lowering his head again.

"Yes, Grozzies . . . a strange people living under the Marshes in some sort of kingdom there. And there Mungo has reappeared as their king. It also seems he's using these folk to build rockets and things to fire at the sun and moon and blot them out. When the world up here is in darkness, then he plans to bring up his Grozzies and rule us."

"What confounded cheek!" murmured Rachel to her neighbour Vicky Vole.

"He'll have to get past me first!" roared Big Bill.

"And I'll make sure he's put out, too, if he tries to put out the sun and moon! I'll put him into permanent orbit up there out of harm's way," said Frisk Otter.

"What a splendid idea," murmured the owl thoughtfully. "I must consider that a little more."

Then Horatio called them to order and they fell silent.

"I must confess I'd forgotten there were such things as Grozzies," Horatio went on. "I thought the rats were simply frightened of some imaginary creature . . . like popinols in our part of Castle Shire. Superstitious old wives' tales and all that. After all, we persuaded them pretty convincingly that *we* were Grozzies when we scooted them through the Tunnel with Hoot's flying-machine. Never for one moment did I really believe they existed. Queer fish they seem, too, by all accounts."

"Excuse me, sir," said Pip timorously, "but they aren't fish. They're more like Humanfolk, 'cept they've only one eye and thick hairy bodies; and they're sort of . . . well, slurpy in all they do and speak, specially when they speak. They're not like fish at all."

"Quite so, quite so, my dear boy," said Horatio gently, patting the fieldmouse on the head. "It was just a figure of speech. I simply meant they were odd when I called them 'queer fish.' "

The only figures Pip knew much about were in sums. He hadn't heard of them in speech before, so he kept quiet. He didn't always understand what the Great Beyonders were saying, but they were such well-meaning folk, and that's all that counts in life. He'd always been brought up to judge folk the way they behaved and treated others; not by how they spoke. Anyhow, among well-meaning folk language isn't spoken, but felt. And when it's felt, it's universally understood.

Bill Badger wanted to know more about the Grozzies; how big they were, how strong, how they grozzified, and so forth.

Rachel Water-Rat also took a keen interest in them. She'd been a key figure in an earlier adventure when they'd "sprung" Nero Squinks from prison. She and Vicky Vole were first-class counter-intelligence agents and had been trained years before in undercover work against Mungo Brown when he'd brought in the Wasteland rats to occupy the Great Beyond. They wanted to know how the Grozzies dressed, how they spoke, what secret passwords they had. Although they looked like ordinary, everyday Animalfolk girls, they were, in fact, very clever and sophisticated detectives; part of an intricate network which protected the Great Beyond from any surprise attack such as Mungo had once carried out.

Pip gave an excellent description. He hadn't missed one detail, for the Grozzies had imprinted themselves firmly in his mind forever. Finally he said, "Though they're clearly very powerful in body, I got the impression they weren't very bright."

"That often follows," said Hoot to himself, but was overheard by Big Bill Badger.

"Not always though," grunted burly Bill.

"Present company excepted," replied the owl quickly. "It's really most rude of me to think aloud. Worse than speaking aloud before you think. What I meant to say was that folk who are physically powerful but don't put their strength to good use are often not very bright. They've let their minds go to seed . . . and the seed has fallen on very stony ground, so that their bodies grow at the expense of their brains. Now, folk who are strong *and* good . . . well, that's another matter altogether. Their bodies do what their brains tell 'em, and that's what brains are for in the first place. Tu-woo!"

Having delivered himself of these pearls of wisdom, the owl looked apologetically over his specs at Bill. The badger agreed, but couldn't help remarking, "Yet there have been times when your brains, Hoot, have needed our bodies, eh?"

"Tu-woo, indeed," conceded the owl. And there the matter rested.

"The question I'd like to ask," said Brushy Fox, "is how on earth these Grozzies came to be under the earth? Who are they?"

He sat back, looking round for an answer. None came. Everybody looked blank. "A good question," said the cat. "Who are they?" As usual it was to the owl they turned for some kind of answer. Hoot said nothing. Then he took off his spectacles and wiped them slowly, a sure sign that something had surfaced in his wise, old head.

He gave his specs a final wipe, then put them on, looking round before saying, "Somewhere in the distant past, I remember my great-great-uncle Barny writing about Grozzies. He once read a paper on Grozziology to the Folkological Society which used to meet here at the castle during the winter. He was a great friend, Horatio, of your great-great-uncle Claudius for they were both keen students of Folkology . . . that is the study of folks," he added by way of explanation, as there were many blank stares facing him. "Somewhere in this library," he continued, "there ought to be a book on the subject. Both of them published their papers, and they did much research into the matter over the years."

"Great-great-uncle Claudius's books are over there," said Horatio, pointing to a distant corner of the room. "Next to my grandfather Tiberius's collection." He went to the collection and raised a pair of stand-steps to get to the top shelf. "Yes, here they are. A bit dusty, I'm afraid. Folkology isn't much in my line so they haven't been read in years."

When Horatio had come down, Hoot mounted the steps, running his wing eagerly along the spines of several ancient volumes and reading aloud their titles. " 'Odd Folk in Humanland,' 'Strange Folk in the Great Beyond,' 'Odder Folk in Humanland' . . . We're getting closer.

Humanland seemed to be a happy hunting ground for their folkological research. Ah, there it is, 'Oddest of Oddities in Humanfolk,'" he exclaimed triumphantly, pulling out a huge, leather-bound book and blowing the dust from it. He opened it and turned to the index. " 'Grozzies and their Origins' by Sir Claudius Fitzworthy and Professor Barnabus Owl," said Hoot.

He brought the book to the table, and they clustered round as he opened its yellowing pages. The ancient casing was cracked, and a very musty smell rose when the owl turned over the pages. He read at length, turning to selected parts of the book which explained about the Grozzies. They all stared in wonder at the strange illustrations of Grozzies and Grozzieland.

"So, my friends," said the owl at length, "it seems we're up against a long-lost race of Humanfolk whose bodies took over their minds, and whose bodies are now being taken over by fungi. Long ago they closed their minds to what was beautiful and lovely up here. They went sulking into the earth, the depths which their minds were fixed on. Now their bodies are changing into something repulsive and evil. Because they saw nothing good in our world of light, their two eyes began to change first. So now they have only one eye to grope and blunder about in their underworld. There, no light penetrates to brighten their lives, except the sad light they give out from inside themselves, which is harmful to others. Without doubt, Mungo has taken them over, exploiting them to work his own evil purposes. Friends, he must be stopped!"

"Hear, hear!" said Brushy Fox. "We've done it before and we'll do it again!" He banged the table defiantly to hammer home his point.

"We'll set off straight away and . . . and blog him!" shouted Big Bill Badger.

The others agreed, shouting noisily, "Yes, to Grozzieland and blog 'em!"

"If we march down the mineshaft quickly, we'll be on 'em before they know what's hit 'em," said Frisk Otter.

"Blog 'em before they realise they've been blogged," backed up the badger.

"Nobble 'em before they know," said Olive Otter.

"Penetrate their intelligence and confound them," added Rachel Water-Rat.

And they all agreed that that was the best course of action . . . all except the owl. He sat mute and waited till they'd done. His silences spoke volumes, and their excited chatter faded away when they realised, one by one, that Hoot wasn't speaking. They knew that when he spoke again, he'd prove them wrong. He always did.

"We shouldn't be thinking about how *quickly* we get them," he said. "We should concentrate on how *best* we tackle the problem. The method of attack you've suggested is exactly what Mungo expects us to do. He wants us all to charge down there so we'll be grozzified. He can do with us what he wants then. And it won't be very pleasant. We'd be in the soup . . . at least, those of us who've been chosen as soup. Please, gentlemen, we must work out a proper plan of campaign, attack the Grozzies where they least expect. I suggest we all go home and think this thing out quietly. You know our combined brainpower always succeeds . . . that is, if we use it together sensibly and coolly. Mungo will do nothing till he has us in his clutches. The sun and moon are quite safe till he has us in his trap."

"Hoot's right," said Horatio. "We must put on our thinking caps. 'Festina lente' Great-great-uncle Claudius always used to say when he got older. We must follow his advice. 'Hurry slowly.' That way we're sure to succeed."

They agreed and the animals set off home. They returned the next day to begin their adventure when they'd thought things over more carefully. Quill stayed the night with Horatio, but Pip needed to explain about the mineshaft in more detail, so that Hoot's master-robot, Charley, could be programmed at Owl View. He went home with Hoot, who borrowed old Sir Claudius's book. "It'll save my robots a great deal of searching if I can show it to them," he explained, saying he'd return it to the library the next day.

Carrying the Folkology book carefully under his wing, Hoot and Pip departed, escorted by Horatio as far as the drawbridge. There he wished them and his other guests goodnight as they trooped home in the dusk.

Chapter 7

Back in Grozzieland, Mungo was becoming more and more edgy. He'd expected the Great Beyonders to appear for some time, but no one had turned up. At the very least, he'd hoped Quill Hedgehog would have been his prisoner by now. All that had happened was a Grozzy patrol had found a basket of mushrooms in one of the upper levels . . . an empty basket by the time it arrived back at headquarters. He was furious with them!

They stood at attention in front of him as he paced back and forth in his operations room, where he kept the maps and records of what was happening in Grozzieland. From time to time he ate cooked toadstools and raw fish from a plate. The fish were strange things, descendants of fish found in the Lonely Lake, deep in the lowest part of Grozzieland. Ages before, sad fish had swum down there and got trapped. In time they'd become colourless and blind, totally white and without eyes. Nevertheless, Mungo found them quite tasty.

"Captain Coniophora Cerebella!" growled Mungo, flicking a fishy paw.

"Yes, your majesty," answered the captain, slopping to attention.

"I can't understand why you found no one in the upper levels where you discovered this mushroom basket. Someone must have put it there. Baskets don't go wandering off on their own," said the cat.

"I can assure you, sir, that we found nothing at all. Not a trace," hissed the Grozzy, emphasising the last sibilant so much he was still hissing a minute later.

"Strange, very strange," murmured Mungo. "I wonder if it's some kind of deception, a way of putting us off their real plans. Why should anyone want to go planting a basket of mushrooms down here? The only thing I can think of, it must have been a Grozzy who'd sneaked out at night to collect 'em, then panicked when he heard you lot coming."

"That must be it, sir," agreed the captain, glad to seize on any excuse which would get him out of trouble. "I'm sure that must be it. You're so clever, your majesty. You think of everything. We'd never have thought of that. Not in a flowing of Grozziedays."

You'll understand that as the moon didn't shine in Grozzieland, there could be no months. They counted their time by the flowing of the Deep River into the Lonely Lake past two pillars of rock. A 'flowing' took about twenty-five days and a Grozzieday lasted twenty-seven and a half hours.

Mungo quietened down. Flattery always soothed him, for he was very prone to it like the rest of us. "Well, I don't want more mistakes like that. No one, I repeat, absolutely no one is to leave the lower levels until further notice. Only the patrols go higher. I want to know the minute any stranger enters my kingdom. When we've taken prisoner all those 'guests' I'm expecting . . . all those fat badgers and cats and hedgehogs, you understand . . . then, oh, what feasties we're going to have! And with no sun and no moon up above, life for us there will be one long feastie."

The Grozzies became excited and chanted, "All praise to King Mungo! All glory to the Supreme King of Grozzieland!" which tickled the cat no end. He simply loved to bask in their chants. Then they fell in front of him, grovelling and slobbering wildly at the mouth.

When he'd had enough, Mungo said, "Get up," and gave the nearest Grozzy an encouraging kick. "Get up, you lot, and come here. I want you to take in these maps. Listen carefully to what I tell you."

The Grozzies stopped grovelling and climbed slowly to their feet, watching Mungo run his paw over the maps. "I've now got my two rockets in position which are going to blast the sun and moon," he said, "They can be fired at any time, at any time I wish, but I won't start the countdown till all my enemies are in my grasp. Oh, no. I want them all to see how clever I am and to be quite sure who will rule Mellowmark, Domusland, and the Great Beyond, when they've been eaten; who will one day rule the world ... even the Humanfolk! I want to have the pleasure of seeing them realise Mungo has outsmarted them all!" Here the evil cat chuckled diabolically ... and the dia was very bolical, indeed. When he'd done, he slipped another oily fish into his mouth and scrunched it noisily, bones and all.

Mungo was beginning to think more and more slowly like the Grozzies, had he known it. Between his words, there were longer and longer intervals. His top-piece was screwing up. The effects of the fungi were catching up on him fast. Had he had the good manners or even the commonsense to realise it, he was about to be rescued from his own evil by those he considered enemies.

He chobbled another plate of toadstools, and wiped his paws on his gown. Then he began fingering the great, gold rings on his fingers, looked at himself in one of the many mirrors, adjusted his crown, and began strolling round the room admiring himself. He purred for some minutes, telling himself what a great guy he was as he looked in his mirrors. And when he'd admired himself enough, he turned back to his henchmen who'd stood round silently, bowing and scraping each time he passed, like heavy wallpaper rolling off the walls.

He pointed to a map on the table. "I expect my enemies to enter here or there," he said. "The fools blew up my master tunnel years ago, so they can come into Grozzieland only by these routes. You must keep constant watch on them, and, above all, when you've captured any prisoner, he must be brought here alive. Understand?"

The cat's eyes flashed beneath his glasses to drive home his point and the Grozzies shuffled nervously. They didn't like his eyes to flash so.

"Most assuredly your will shall be done, Great Mungo," hissed Captain Cerebella, and the others sizzled assent behind him.

"Good!" retorted Mungo. "Then let me hear you repeat the formula I've tried to instil into your fat brains. What do you do when you capture anyone?"

The patrols lined before the cat and chorused, "One. We must grozzify all intruders at once. Two. We must bring them back unharmed—and uneaten. Three. We must report captures to All-gracious Mungo. Four. We must put all prisoners in the cells . . . ready for microwaving!" They said the last instruction with obvious relish and slopped and splurted for seconds after, then they flopped to the floor and grovelled.

Mungo let them wallow a while before ordering them up. Then he said simply, "And then?"

"Then we eatsies and feasties!" they said gleefully, rubbing their tummies and smacking their lips most moistly. Mungo smiled as he watched the feeble-minded creatures. They made him feel great, tiny-minded as he himself was. His head had swelled noticeably since his stay with them. He looked very much like a bloated toadstool when he wore his crown—one of the red and yellow varieties. He liked his crown so much, incidentally, he'd even taken to wearing it in bed as a kind of comforter.

When he'd finished briefing the four leading Grozzies, he ordered them to barracks. There, they sent the Grozzies under their command out on patrol as Mungo strolled to the dungeons, where Mick, Mack, and Nero grew more despondent by the hour.

The sadder they became, the more pleased grew Mungo. It was part of his wicked nature to torment and bully, so he enjoyed watching them suffer. They sat back to back in abject dismality, the worst state of being dismal. Nero's eye was dull, and though he was the supreme optimist, there was always the suspicion of a tear lurking in its corner. The others snivelled openly. Mick had gone into the moult and Mack had lost a great deal of weight. Neither were the jolly policemen they'd been a few weeks earlier.

"It don't look as though we're goin' to get out o' this scrape this time," said Mack. "We've been abandoned. We oughter heard something by now, but I think there ain't nothing nobody can do to help . . . nohow."

"Nowhere," said Mick.

"No time," concluded Nero.

Their dirge continued.

"An' if they do try to snatch us, they'll only get nabbed themselves," said Mack.

"Somewhere," said Mick.

"Some time," agreed Nero.

"It's 'cos Grozzies ain't natural they got us beat. They don't act natural anymore," said Mack.

"Anywhere," seconded Mick.

"Anytime," moaned Nero.

"Humanfolk ain't really natural anyhow," Mack went on. "It's my belief it's from them Mungo gets all his crazy ideas about money an' power. It ain't natural at all . . . leastways, not in our part of the world. So we can't escape.

We can only wait to be eaten . . . or worse, put in as flavouring for pies."

A loud laugh outside their door startled them and cut short their dirge. But it didn't lighten their hearts one jot. On the contrary, it made them sadder. Mungo had arrived. He let himself into their cell with gusto. He knew he was quite safe, for they were shackled. "And very fine flavouring you'll make," he said breezily. Though it was dark, he lit up with dull Grozzy light. And by it, the trio noticed another peculiar thing, something which had started to happen after they'd arrived in Grozzieland. His eyes were growing closer together. They seemed to be moving upwards to join into one over the bridge of his noise. Moreover he slurred his words more and more, hissing slovenly like his subjects. He was becoming a Grozzy rapidly!

Unaware of this, he began to speak. "Yes, earthlings, you've landed right in the soup this time. At least two of you have. They're rather partial to magpie soup down here. You'll have the honour of being served first, for our feasties are very formal. We dine in the correct order like the gentlefolks we are. Soup followed by releves and removes. The voles and fieldmice are reserved for those. Then the entrées . . . mole paté and otter paste. Delightful! Delightful!" And here the wicked cat showed another Grozzy feature. He smacked his lips loudly. "Then we come to you, Nero Squinks . . . pie, rat-pie. And a fine pie you'll make, eyeshade and all. 'Ratty-tatty Pie' the Grozzies call it. You'll go down a treat. With his prickles, Quill Hedgehog may be a little sharp, but they'll relish the badger. Plenty of him to go round, too. As for Hoot Owl, he'll certainly give them food for thought!" He watched the effects of his words sink in, before working himself up to describe what was to happen to his arch-enemy, Horatio Fitzworthy. "But what won't we do to that aristocratic fool Fitzworthy?

65

I'll have him trussed and roasted slowly over hot charcoal, barbecued and basted in his own grounds at Fitzworthy Castle to celebrate our arrival once more in the world above. I'll enjoy every mouthful of kebabbed cat!"

"You . . . you cannibal!" was all Nero could utter.

"You're nothing more than a Grozzy alley cat!"

"Right in one way, wrong in another. I'm not an alley cat. I'm King of the Grozzies, and as such I have to fit in with their ways and tastes. And once we've eaten you, you'll be one of us, so to speak. You'll all be incorporated members of Grozzieland, part of the body of our realm."

Mungo laughed loud and long at his terrible jokes, and his mad laugh trailed behind as he clanged the cell-door closed. It was heard echoing and re-echoing, following him down the corridor.

"Oh, my poor feathers!" wailed Mick, as several of those attachments fell out each time he shivered. "That alley cat will be the death of me!"

"You can count us all in on that," said Mack dismally. "The only comfort I get from the whole blooming business is that there won't be anything left of me to eat by the time they've finished. That'll give me some sort of pleasure before I goes."

"Except you won't be here to enjoy it," commented Nero.

"I'd rather be here as nothing than as a Grozzy potboiler. How long we been in this place now?" Mack asked.

The rat lifted his chains and carried them to the wall. In the flickering light of his lantern, he could make out a row of notches he'd cut. He screwed his eyes, when he felt them to count with his forefinger.

"Three weeks, two days," he said. "Almost a month. You'd have thought someone would have showed up by now. Very strange," he mused, before repeating, "Very strange." And he sank so deep in thought the others imagined he'd dozed off. But so deep was he turning over something in his mind, that when what subsequently happened did happen, it didn't come as much as a surprise to Nero as it did to Mick and Mack.

Chapter 8

When Hoot and Pip left the castle, they went to the Wood. In the middle, Hoot had his home, Owl View. As the two creatures plodded on side by side, Hoot carrying Sir Claudius Fitzworthy's book, and Pip walking very respectfully in step, the owl explained all about the Grozzies and their subterranean kingdom. Pip was fascinated, and not a little scared of what the owl said. He was glad he hadn't known about them so much when he'd seen them at first. He might not have gone into that mineshaft knowing what he knew now. So engrossed was he in what the owl said, he scarcely noticed darkness fall as they moved further into the Wood.

Finally, they stopped beneath a huge oak tree at the foot of which was a sign 'Owl View' and a little notice inviting callers to pull the bell-rope and wait for an answer. Owl View hadn't changed much since the day Quill had stumbled into it pursued by the Wastelanders. Of course, the bell-rope and notice weren't there then, because Owl View had to remain secret and hidden, had to look like an ordinary tree, and that's why Quill had been saved.

It still looked very much like an oak from the outside. And that's a curious thing, isn't it? Animals' homes look like trees or riverbanks or holes in the ground or whatever, but once you enter them, well, that's a different mat-

Police-cadet Pip dines with Quill, Hoot, and Horatio

69

ter. Perhaps it's to keep away our prying Humanfolk eyes that the Animalfolk disguise their homes so effectively.

Hoot pulled the bell-rope. Deep within the oak a mellow chime rang. There was a moment's silence, then to Pip's amazement a secret door opened in the side of the oak. More than that, a strange machine stood just inside and invited them to enter in very mechanical yet very cultured tones. They were also kindly. "Good evening, sir," it said to Hoot, who invited Pip in.

"Good evening, Charley," said the owl. "This is my friend Pip Fieldmouse, Police-cadet Fieldmouse. He'll be staying overnight, so would you prepare a room for him, please, and rustle up a meal for us?"

"Of course, sir. Welcome to Owl View, Mr. Pip," said the robot. "May I take your hat, sir?"

Pip was a bit thrown. Rather awkwardly he handed his hat to the robot, from which a steely arm had appeared out of a control-box. The fieldmouse didn't know what to do or say. He'd never met a robot before, certainly not such a couth one as this. It was a gentleman; indeed, it was more. It was a gentleman's gentleman, the owl's butler and right-hand man.

A light flashed on its head, but once they'd gone inside, the light stopped and the door slid silently behind them. They were in an ante-chamber of some sort, and before them was a heavily studded door. It looked centuries old, as though it had come from the lodgegate of a castle. There were a lantern and matches, which seemed a little out of place in such a computerised setting and handled by a robot. When Charley had lit the lantern, he let them in.

"I love old things," remarked the owl. "That's why I try to keep my place balanced . . . the old and new side by side. They blend time. Old things have as much to offer as the new, as much to tell us. They keep us in touch with the past and lead us to the future, which can't be the future unless it has the past to back it up. Together they make the present."

Pip got a little lost with what the owl said, but he thought he understood when he'd turned it over a bit in his mind. Years later he understood completely. Then he just nodded. The robot went ahead, moving noiselessly up a spiral staircase till it reached a door some way above them. They followed more leisurely, stopping every now and then to look at oil portraits, several of which hung on the wall. They were Hoot's academic ancestors, all of them very learned owls weighty with wisdom and knowledge.

"This is my great-great-uncle Barny," he said, pausing beneath an owl in old-fashioned, academic dress, "the expert on Folkology. He worked many years with old Sir Claudius Fitzworthy recording the customs and speech of the Mellowmarkians. A great scholar Uncle Barny . . . tu-woo," said the owl, giving a little hoot of admiration. "Alas, he went off alone one day into the Mystery Marshes and never returned. All they found was his spectacles . . . perhaps that's why it says in the history books he came to a spectacular end, because the Grozzies got him and ate him. He disappeared without so much as a hoot."

Pip shivered. He'd seen Grozzies and his imagination needed no further prompting about Professor Barnabus Owl's end.

"Still," continued Hoot as they started climbing the steps again, "he managed to record much information about them before that fateful last trip, and we'll find it most useful."

At the end of the long line of family portraits hung more recent ones of Hoot's nephew and sister. He paused before the photograph of his younger sister, an academic owl like himself, though rather less severe-looking than Hoot. Clearly Hoot was very fond of her. "This is my sister," he said proudly; then nodding at the adjacent portrait, "And that is her son. They branched out into engineering. She's Dr. Tu-whoot Owl." He turned and looked roguishly at Pip for a moment before saying, "Because it was rumoured my father once said he didn't give two hoots whether she was a boy or a girl owl, as long as she was a scholarly owl. As it transpired she was a girl owl *and* scholarly, so his casual observation became a by-word in the family, and her name. A most accomplished owlette, my sister Tu-whoot," he concluded.

All the while, Pip said never a word. He followed the owl and listened. Occasionally they passed doors where peculiar sounds emerged; and other doors from which peculiar smells came, strange chemical smells with strange chemical sounds, glugging and gurgling and bubbling. He also caught glimpses of flasks and chemical apparatus by the metre.

Eventually they reached the owl's study, a huge room lined with books, and papers spilling everywhere, from the bookshelves onto tables, even the floor. There were maps and plans, and under one window a fine draughtsman's drawing-board and set. Another strange machine stood by Hoot's desk, and Pip had nicely settled in a comfortable chair, when a robot voice came from the machine saying, "Care for some tea, sir?"

Like Quill and Kraken the Raven before him, Pip jumped, rather as I do when my alarm-clock goes off. By reflex he answered, "Er . . . yes, please, that's very kind of you." The machine bubbled gently in acknowledgement.

"Not at all, sir," it said. "The pleasure's entirely mine."

There was more bubbling and sizzling, then within seconds two ready-made cups of tea were produced from inside the machine, served on the machine's long, steely arms. Milk and sugar followed and finally the tea-robot asked, "Care for biscuits, sir?"

"Rather," said Pip, for he was feeling quite peckish after his long walk.

At once a selection of biscuits was offered. He chose two chocolate and three ginger biscuits, for he was a growing lad. Hoot picked a ginger biscuit and dunked it in his tea, as all ginger biscuits should be eaten. Then he munched thoughtfully.

The more he munched, the more engrossed he became in some plans and a map on his desk. Pip had eaten his ginger biscuits and was tucking into the first of the chocolate ones before Hoot spoke again. The robot drew his attention to his guest. Charley gave a discreet cough and when Hoot looked up, the robot nodded in Pip's direction.

"Oh, do forgive me," said the owl. "It's very bad manners to ignore you as I am doing, but I got rather into these plans. I drew them up a short time ago. I believe they're exactly what we need for getting into Grozzieland unobserved. Come over hear and I'll explain them to you."

Pip was about to leave his chair, but Hoot said, "No, stay put. There's no need to get up. Just press the blue button on your control panel. It's on the arm of your chair . . . and the chair will do the rest."

Dumbfounded, the fieldmouse did as he was told. No sooner had he pressed the button than the chair began to move, carrying him smoothly round the desk to Hoot's side. "A most useful chair," commented Hoot. "Especially when I've got a twinge of rheumatics in my toes. I suffer from them occasionally after sitting on damp branches. Now if you'd care to look over this drawing here, I'll explain it to you. This is a plan of my new submarine, the Hootasub Mark 2. I invented it to take a closer look at the pondlife in Fitzworthy Moat. I'm too old now for aqualung diving and all that sort of thing, but with my Hootasub I can go to the bottom of the moat or the river and examine things underwater as long as I like. With a

73

few adjustments, it should take all of us to Grozzieland and we can come at Mungo where he least expects us."

The fieldmouse peered at the blueprint and listened carefully to Hoot. The two explained everything clearly, and Pip marvelled at his inventiveness more and more. When he'd done, Hoot turned to the map.

"Charley did very well finding this," he said. "I never knew we had it in the mappery."

It was an extremely old and yellow map, crumbling at the edges and drawn by a Humanfolk called John Speede. Pip had to look very close to make out the writing on it, which was thin and spidery. Its title read, "A New and accurat map of the World drawne according to ye truest Descriptions latest Discoveries & best Observations yat have beene made by English or Strangers. 1651." There were signs of the sun and moon eclipses in its bottom corners and all sorts of wonderful pictures and detail on it. At the bottom of one side of the map was "Unknown Land." It was here that Hoot pointed.

"Here is where we live," he said, as he drew out another very old and decrepit map with Domusland, the Great Beyond, Mellowmark, and Mereful on, as well as all Animalfolk lands then known. "The Humanfolk haven't discovered us yet," said the owl. "So an ancestor of mine had to draw this map to show where Grozzieland is in our Animalfolk world."

"It's certainly very ancient," observed Pip.

"Yet a most accurate example of cartography considering when it was made," said Hoot.

"Please," said the fieldmouse in a small voice, "what's cart . . . what you said?"

"Cartography? Oh, it's simply map-making, though map-making is far from simple. That's why they give it a difficult name," replied the owl. "They do that with difficult things. Now, do you know Mellowmark?"

74

"Yes," said Pip. "I've been there many times with Sergeant Mack to see Elderman Squinks. I know the part
which borders Domusland very well."

"Then you'll recognise the Great Mere of Mellowmark
here," said Hoot, pointing to a stretch of faded blue on
the map. The fieldmouse nodded. "Now, there's always
been a mystery connected with the water of the Great
Mere. Nobody knows where it goes, for a river flows from
it at the southern end. For a long time everyone assumed
it drained into the Mystery Marshes and then into the
Hazy River which empties into the Windy Sea. But I've a
theory . . . only a theory, mind . . . that the water, or some
of it, goes into a vast underground lake, the Lonely Lake."

"The Lonely Lake? I've never heard of it," said Pip.

"Neither had I till this morning when I was looking
through Sir Claudius's and Uncle Barny's books. Then,
tu-woo! It struck me all at once." Here the owl turned
excitedly to the book he'd brought from Horatio's library
and opened it at a map of Grozzieland. His eyes twin-
kled behind his glasses as he placed the open book side
by side with the ancient map. "There," he said proudly,
"there. The two match up exactly. One's on top, and the
other's underneath. That's all. But I'm running ahead of
myself as usual," he apologised. "Have another cup of
tea and I'll explain."

The tea-robot trundled round to Pip and topped him
up. It saw that his biscuits had vanished, too, so handed
him another plateful.

"My robots have all turned out such good boys," he
said. "It's been a great relief to me and I'm very proud of
them. You see so many going off the rails these days, when
folk like Mad Mungo begin programming them."

He paused because the tea-robot had begun brewing
another pot of tea inside himself and the noise of bubbling and boiling filled the air. The owl reached for another

Charley serves tea and biscuits to Pip and Hoot

biscuit and dreamily nibbled at it while surveying the blueprint before him. He absent-mindedly began feeling for his tea-cup to dunk his biscuit in and the robot helped him out by providing another cuppa.

"Thank you," said the owl, looking up. "I'm most grateful. You know, my robots look after me as if I were their father . . . which, on reflection, I suppose I am."

Replenished in cup and crunchy, the two creatures poured over maps and plans till well into the night. At one stage, Hoot brought in his map-making robot, Mat, who drew them a splendid new map of the mine-workings from the description Pip gave, much in the way he'd drawn a map from what Kraken had told him years before.

"Going through the Lonely Lake is the only safe way in," said Hoot. "If we try going down the old mineshafts, they'll be ready for us. Surprise is what counts. We don't want that blighter firing off his rockets at all costs . . . nor do we want grozzifying. However," he concluded, rolling up his map carefully and putting it away, "if we pop up where we're least expected, bang in the middle of the Lonely Lake, they're ours for the taking."

He handed his map to Charley who locked it away in the map-drawer. Pip gave a huge yawn, despite himself, and set off Hoot. There was a quiet buzz from Charley, a robot-yawn, for his light had grown appreciably dimmer.

"It's time we turned in," said Hoot. "It's well past my bedtime . . . and yours, too, young man. Charley, please take Pip to his room. There's no great need for us to be up early, so don't set your alarm too soon."

Charley's blue light flashed several times as he registered what Hoot said. "Points understood and recorded," he replied. "Now, Police-cadet Pip, if you follow me, I'll take you to your room. The tea-robot will serve you something tonight if you want a bed-time drink. He'll come with us and stay in your room, won't you, old Tea-leaves?" The tea-robot sizzled his reply and went with them.

Pip thanked Hoot and after wishing him goodnight, followed Charley up the wooden stairs to a tiny guest-room near the top of the tree. Charley asked him if there was anything else he needed, then wished him goodnight, leaving Pip with Tea-leaves, the tea-robot. Old Tea-leaves also made cocoa and brewed up a cup for Pip's goodnight drink, then he switched off and settled down for the night.

Pip snuggled deep into the crisp, fresh, linen sheets Charley had put on the bed. Outside, the full moon peered through the latticework. The strong arms of the oak shook gently and numerous twigs and leaves rustled soothingly, hanging sleep more heavily on the fieldmouse's lids with each shake. If you'd have counted the seconds it took for Pip to drop off, starting from the moment he finished his drink and snuggled down the bed, I doubt if you'd have got past ten.

Chapter 9

The shock of capture left Nero and the magpies when they'd been held prisoner for a couple of months. They got used to a daily routine, and they got used to the Grozzies ... as far as you can feel at home with such beings. Once they knew they were not to be eaten, that nothing would happen to them till Quill and the others appeared, they felt much more at ease. Despair never quite left them, but Nero's optimism returned and infected the other two. They began making plans to escape.

All of them had become very thin, so the Grozzies decided they needed better food to fatten them up ready for the final beanfeast. More normal food was given, and this cheered them immensely, particularly Mack. As they fattened, so they grew more friendly with their guards; at least, their guards became much more interested in them. Captain Coniophora and his comrades slurped their way each day to the dungeon simply to look at their future feasties and smack their thick lips.

At first, this was somewhat off-putting, but gradually Nero and the rest got used to it. Indeed, after a while, they built up quite a relationship with their guards. It must have been the only friendship ever between diners and dinners. Few people make friends with their meal before it's cooked, but the Grozzies did with Nero, Mack, and Mick.

It was a kind of apertif friendship, a pre-dinner togetherness before they all went into dine . . . or be dined on. The Grozzy guards greeted their new friends more and more warmly each time they met, putting their arms round them and calling them all sorts of endearing names. They'd begun to call them 'feastie friends' very early on. "They're seeing how plump we're getting, that's all," said Mack. "Feeling if we're oven-ready when they put their arms round us, ugh! Still, if they feed us as well as they're filling us now, it's better than being put in the pot a bag of bones and boiled for stock. I don't mind 'em eating well off me, as long as they lets me eat well first."

So friendly had they become with their guards, that each evening the four Grozzy commanders trooped down to their cell and talked with them. They regarded them as edible pets and, more important, they found that Mick, Mack, and Nero amused them, taught them new tricks and told them good tales. You must remember the Grozzies had been cut off from our world a long time and had forgotten most of the things you and I take for granted, which make us happy.

Take the card-game Snap, for example. No Snap had been played in Grozzieland. They'd no amusing card or party-games that we have in our bright world. Grozzy lives were dull. They'd seen little good in the world they'd left so long before, and now their lives were very, very dull by our standards.

It's true they did have parties and dances of a kind, but they were extraordinarily dull occasions. Feasties formed the centre of their activities . . . and we certainly wouldn't have found them appetising. Just the opposite. Their dances were boring in the extreme. They simply jogged slowly up and down to a terrible row made by a 'group' or 'backing' which were first-class headache-makers but couldn't produce music. They sort of jogged in front of each other not talking, because the racket was so loud.

The lights from their eyes flashed on and off, and altogether the noise and atmosphere were horrendous, particularly if they'd dined on toadstools first.

As the 'dance' or 'grozzigigue' (as they called it) dragged on, their lights began to fade. They stopped then, else they'd never have been able to find their way home in the dark, sloshing and squelching back to the miserable caves they called 'homes.' 'Dens' would have been a better name for them.

So it was something of an occasion when three lively characters like Mick, Mack, and Nero were able to entertain them; and being the selfish creatures they were, the Grozzy commanders kept them all to themselves. They didn't want anyone else to share their fun. Mack had a whole fund of improbable stories he spun, and they believed every word! Mick played his tin whistle and Nero thought about singing . . . then he thought again. He didn't want to antagonise his guards. They might have grozzified him permanently. Instead, he showed them how to dance, for he was quite good at jigs and reels and all those traditional dances which enlighten our world. He showed them how to hornpipe, for they were highly attracted to dancing and Mick's playing, even though their own music was so primitive. They weren't much good at dancing anything complicated like a jig or hornpipe, but they tried hard, floundering about in a heavy-footed way trying to copy Nero's delicate steps.

"It's not easy!" gasped Sergeant Merulius Lacrymans, flopping wearily onto a bed in their cell after a dance practice.

"It's too complicated!" wheezed Sergeant Daedalia Quercina, staggering to another bed, his one eye shut tight with fatigue. Yet he had tried. Like all the Grozzies, he was fascinated by music.

Nero observed them closely. It was the speed and ease with which they became tired, and the tightness they

81

closed their eyes with, which gave him an idea for escape. So one evening, when Captain Cerebella and his pals had gone, Nero explained his plan.

"We'll get 'em playing Snap first," he said, "then, when they start quarrelling, which they always do, we'll start 'em dancing . . . first we'll dance 'em out, then we'll dance ourselves out of this hole."

"What d'you mean?" asked Mick.

"We use their quarrelling at Snap to make 'em dance . . . get 'em seeing who's best at dancing. Then dance 'em out," said Nero.

"Ah, I gets you," said Mick as light dawned. "We plays on their pride, makes 'em dance an' when they flops on our beds . . ."

"We grab their keys," continued Nero.

"An' scarper!" concluded Mack. "That's great! What a mind you've got Nero Squinks! You'd make a first-class copper."

Nero coughed modestly and looked down. "I was in the prison line once, remember? I didn't make such a good showing then."

"That's all in the past. We was all what we shouldn't have been then," said Mack, putting a friendly arm round him. Then they began to chatter at once, suggesting this and planning that for escaping and getting clear of Grozzieland.

Nero drew a map of Grozzieland in the dust on the floor. From what they'd gleaned from the guards, he'd worked out where the tunnels and mineshafts were, the exits and entrances to their kingdom, and then he'd worked out how they could escape.

"There's one drawback, though," said Mack at length.

"What's that?" asked Nero in surprise. "I don't see how we can go wrong once we're through that door. I'm sure I know the way right across Grozzieland now to the old mineshafts."

"It's them rockets . . . the rockets what Mungo's built," he said. "If ever he lets 'em off, it don't matter whether we escape or not. Once the sun and moon's out, he'll capture us again up there. Then we'll be worse off than ever . . . and everyone else."

Nero sighed. "I was forgetting about those," he said, looking hard at his map in the dust. He remained lost in thought a minute. Then he looked up. The light in his eye told the others he'd thought of something brilliant again. "I've another idea," he continued. "From what we've heard, the rocket-launching pads are about here." He pointed to a gallery not far away from their cell. "If . . . if we could get at those, perhaps we could sabotage 'em."

"We ain't got enough know-how, Nero. We needs someone who knows something about rockets an' all that," said Mack.

As if in answer, there came a soft "tu-woo" outside their cell door.

"You say something?" said Mack, looking across at Mick. "I'd have sworn I heard a owl." He scratched the features on the back of his head, looking puzzled. There was another hoot, this time a little louder.

Nero blinked, and they looked at each other as if they'd *all* hooted. Then Mack said, "Did . . . did you hear what I thought I heard?"

"We did," said Nero. "An' we thought it was you."

"What was it you thought you heard what was me?" he asked.

"A nowl," whispered Mick. "I could have sworn I heard a nowl!"

They looked at the door, wondering if they were hearing things. A third hoot dispelled all doubt. Rushing to the door, they peered through the peep-hole and made out the shape of Hoot Owl, his glasses flashing in the light from their candle. He was standing tip-toe to look in, and he whispered to them to be silent.

"How, how on earth did you get here?" whispered Nero, scarcely able to contain his excitement.

"We didn't come on earth. We came under it . . . under water to be more exact . . . through the Lonely Lake," said the owl.

"Who's we?" asked Mack.

"The Great Beyonders and a couple of Domuslanders, Quill Hedgehog and the admirable young police-cadet you've trained so well, Pip Fieldmouse. He's the one who brought news of your capture. I'll tell you about it later. They're in my Hootasub under the Lonely Lake at present waiting for me to return. I've been trying to track you down with the help of my robot Charley. He located you from your heat-waves. You give off a heat-wave frequency rather different from the Grozzies, though we almost got side-tracked to Mungo Brown at first. You know, he's got a slightly different heat-wave system from the Grozzies, too. Not much, but enough to put us on the wrong scent for a while."

"He's enough to put anyone on the wrong scent, he is," growled Mack. "You can smell him a mile off."

The owl was about to reply, when they heard the slurp-slurp of a Grozzy guard coming down the corridor.

"Alien approaching," warned Charley. "Only sixty metres away."

"If you don't mind," said Hoot quickly, "we'll buzz off for a while. We've been dodging these wretched creatures all day!"

Hoot and Charley slipped off quietly as the Grozzy's light became brighter. Heavy and moist he sloshed up to their door and looked in, checked that his prisoners were secure, licked his lips, then gave them a most unwholesome smile. "Feasties! Feasties!" was all he said. Something like a laugh bubbled in his throat, but sank back before it surfaced. He closed the peep-hole and moved off on his rounds, still giving several of his unriseable laughs.

The trio had long learned to avoid looking directly at a Grozzy's eye and explained this to Hoot and Charley when they came back. They also told Hoot about Mungo's rockets and where he had them.

"They're in a gallery not far from here," said Nero. "He's got 'em all ready to fire as soon as he's collared you lot."

"Then he's got a long wait," said Hoot. "He doesn't know we're here already . . . and that will be our trumpcard . . ."

"Snap!" said Nero suddenly.

"I beg your pardon?" answered the surprised owl on the other side of the door. "What do you mean?"

"We're playing Snap tonight with the Grozzy commanders, and we're going to play our trump-card, too, at Snap," explained the rat, who went on to tell Hoot about their plans for escape.

When he'd done, Hoot said, "Admirable, admirable! A most excellent plan, tu-woo! And once you're free you'll be able to join us under the lake. We can coordinate our plans there for a joint attack on the rocket-base. Now, when will your Grozzy friends be coming back?"

"They return for a game of Snap at seven each night. By eight, we should have 'em nicely tucked up in bed fast asleep," said Nero.

"Good," said Hoot. "Then Charley and I will meet you here tomorrow night at eight o'clock sharp. Once we're on board the Hootasub, you can help me programme Charley with what you know. He'll need your help, won't you?" he said, turning to the robot.

"Affirmative, sir," came back the reply, and the three inside saw Charley's blue light start flashing with excitement as his computers warmed up. He did so enjoy tackling new problems. He began to click loudly till Hoot instructed him to calm down and threw a small switch on the robot's side. "What an adventure this is turning out to be!" said Charley, once his clicking had stopped.

85

"I haven't enjoyed myself so much since I broke the cucumber code three years ago."

"Cucumber code?" echoed Mack, standing on tip-toe to see the robot.

"Oh, it was a little experiment we did together," explained Hoot. "I'm most partial to cucumbers and I was attempting to find some means of growing them all the year round. I needed to crack their bio-code . . . to see if I could cross cucumbers from Australia. They grow there in summer when it's winter over here, you see. I sent Charley on a special flight in Hootaplane Mark 3 to the antipodes and back to gather cucumbers for me. We successfully crossed cucumbers in the Great Beyond with cucumbers from Australia once we'd broken the bio-code. Now we have them all year round in my greenhouse. The only trouble is the Australian part of my cucumbers sometimes comes out and they grow the wrong way up . . . but they taste just as nice despite defying gravity."

Here, the owl glanced at his watch. "We ought to be getting back," he said. "The others may be worrying where we've got to. Charley, you're quite sure you've registered all the information for our return?"

"Affirmative, sir," came back the reply.

"Good, because I've a great deal of map-drawing to do with Mat when we're on board again," said Hoot. "Once we start running up and down the galleries here, we all have to know where we're going. Until tomorrow night then, you folks, goodnight." Then he was off with Charley.

"Goodnight," they replied and watched the light of Charley fade, as he and the owl made their way back to the submarine. And I can't deny the trio in the cell felt very sad as they watched their friends disappear. However, when they'd settled down for the night and were fast asleep, Mack dreamed of freedom for the first time in months . . . and not being eaten by Grozzies!

86

Chapter 10

At seven the next night, Captain Coniophora Cerebella and his companions went to play Snap with the prisoners. They'd had a hard day patrolling the labyrinth of corridors which made up their kingdom and they were tired. They had found no Great Beyonders and it seemed less and less likely that any would appear, despite the rantings of King Mungo, who daily became more and more agitated. He couldn't understand at all why no one had turned up to rescue the rat and magpies. Little did he guess that at that very moment a whole Hootasubful of Great Beyonders, together with Hoot's robots, Charley and Mat, were under the waters of the Lonely Lake right in the heart of Grozzieland. Indeed, Hoot and Charley had already set off to bring back the bait from the trap Mungo thought he'd sprung. They were about to release Nero, Mick, and Mack from the cell, where the Grozzy commanders had gathered.

"We're very tired," said Captain Cerebella, humping through the cell-door followed by the others. "Make us happy. Teach us some gamesies."

Sergeant Daedalia Quercina locked the door and tucked the key securely in his pocket. They'd switched off the grozzification frequency from their light, so that it didn't interfere with the evening's entertainment. They'd at long last cottoned on that if they wanted to have some fun, they had to keep their prisoners conscious, otherwise they were zonked out for the evening. So they switched from grozzifying to a dimmer, less harmful light frequency.

Sergeant Daedalia loved food more than most Grozzies, so he took a special interest in the condition of his captives. He smiled a slow, satisfied smile as he noticed they'd put on weight, for he hadn't been to see them for a while.

"The cook is looking well after you?" he asked heartily.

"Yes," said Mack with much less heartiness. His voice had a very hollow ring about it.

"He gives you everything you need in the eating line then?" enquired Lieutenant Poria Monticola, feeling their arms and legs in a hungry sort of way as he walked round them.

"More than enough," answered Nero, looking at him coldly. He didn't like the lieutenant at all; not that he enjoyed any of the Grozzies' company. But Lieutenant Monticola had a lean and hungry look. He was the sort of person who crept up on you when you were least expecting him. He was dark and swarthy, an unhealthy brownish colour which gave him a crumbly appearance, like a slice of wet, overdone toast.

Captain Coniophora, by way of contrast, was large, disgustingly so. He had a fat face, purple and puffy. Fine, blood-red veins ran over his nose and cheeks like lost lanes on a map. They made him appear more purple than ever, because really he was quite pale underneath. Anger blew him crimson.

They were damper than usual from their long treks underground. They'd tramped miles checking and rechecking the entry points to their kingdom, making sure no one had come in from above. So they were bad-tempered . . . very bad-tempered, and no Grozzy is sweet-tempered even at his best.

"If I've told the guards in Gallery B not to go into Gallery C once, I've told them a dozen times," complained Sergeant Merulius Lacrymans, whining his esses till he sounded like a shower at full pelt.

"And I've had a dreadful day in the lower galleries. Nothing but trouble with the new recruits. They get thicker than ever," added Sergeant Daedalia.

Nero couldn't believe that. No one could be less intelligent than the Grozzy commanders. They were quite the dullest people he'd ever met. They reminded him strongly of shapeless shirts and baggage straight from the washing. They wouldn't have dried even in the hottest sunshine; not that they'd have wanted to. They hated the light in the world above. But though they were dull, they were evil. They were full of low cunning, which is much worse than high cunning.

Mack tried to be pleasant. He shuffled a pack of cards with an ease that betrayed long practice. "Well, what's it to be tonight, gentlemen?" he asked. He knew beforehand what they'd reply, but he always asked them to make them feel important.

"Snap!" they replied together, as they did every night.

"Then Snap it shall be," said Mack, dealing the cards.

"And it's my turn to lead tonight," said Captain Coniophora.

"You *always* lead," complained the lieutenant, who never ceased moaning.

The captain turned slowly and glared angrily at him. "I'm boss here!" he said with authority. "I lead every time. Understand?"

The others looked sulky, grumbling damply under damp breath. Clearly they were in a foul mood and that suited their prisoners. It meant they would finish cards quicker, then Mick could play and dance them to sleep.

89

Mack and the Grozzy commanders play Snap

Mack dealt the cards swiftly, too swiftly for the Grozzies to notice he dealt them similar cards. They studied them hard, then put them slowly on the table, for they couldn't move fast. The captain and lieutenant were the first to set identical cards down, but so slow were they speaking, it was difficult to say who hissed "Snap!" first.

"I was first," said the captain, scooping the cards.

"No, you didn't, sir. Lieutenant Monticola said 'Snap!' before you," complained Merulius, who didn't like to see the captain win unfairly all the time.

"I did!" shouted the captain. "Didn't I, Sergeant Daedalia?" appealing to the sergeant who he knew was keen for promotion.

"By a short 's,' sir, I would say," replied the other, keeping in his captain's good books.

The captain continued scooping the cards, which infuriated the rest.

In the next hand, Mack made sure the captain and lieutenant would call together again.

The lieutenant was so eager to call he essed longer than usual so that the captain finished long before him. He began to collect in his cards and the lieutenant renewed his whining.

" 'Tain't fair," he grumbled, "You win very time. No point in playing if people won't play fair. I'm not going to play any more!"

"Me neither!" supported Lacrymans, as tears of anger filled his eye.

"Then don't play if you don't want to!" snapped the captain. "There's others who like playing. Sergeant Quercina and I will play together. You're just spoil-sports!" And having sprayed his wrath all over Mack, the captain went on playing and the sergeant went on letting him win.

The magpies and rat could scarcely contain their mirth. None dared look the others in the eye for fear of bursting out laughing and ruining their plans. Lieutenant Monticola went several shades darker and sulked with his sergeant, turning to the wall. Meanwhile, the captain won every game till at length even he became bored with winning and asked Mick to play a tune.

The magpie struck up with a lively favourite called "Cock o' the North" and the Grozzies began their dancing. They humped and thumped and floundered about trying to keep time with the jig. Faster and faster played Mick. More and more heavily they danced, slower and slower. At length, it was clear they were played out. Light began to fade from their eyes as perspiration ran in chilly drops all about them. They looked like soggy underwear left on the line in wet weather.

"Stop! Stop!" sobbed Captain Cerebella, fighting for breath.

"Why, you soldiers ain't beat yet, are you?" asked Mack, keeping them hard at it, though he also felt pretty whacked. Nero stuck grimly to his task, out-dancing them all.

"Come, come," he gasped. "We're just beginning to enjoy ourselves. Don't spoil the fun. Can't you Grozzies keep pace with us mere over-earthlings?"

That hurt the Grozzies' pride. They pulled themselves together and went on dancing. They danced for a good half-hour more till Mick's throat felt like a furnace. His lips were dry and raw. His throat burned. He was at his last gasp, then suddenly it happened. All that Nero had guessed came true.

Captain Coniophora Cerebella was the first to go. He was heaviest. He staggered to a bed and flopped, snoring loudly before his head hit the pillow. Once he'd gone, the others followed suit.

"I knew I'd beat him!" gloated the lieutenant. Then he, too, slumped on a bed dead-beat.

The sergeants, who'd been holding each other up, dropped to the floor when their officers packed in. They sat back-to-back, their heads draped over their chests . . . and the snores they gave had to be heard to be believed. They roared and blew like foghorns till the cell began to shake.

"Quick," said Nero. "Let's get out of here before their noise brings the guards!"

The moment Sergeant Quercina dropped, Mack lifted his cell-key. They raced to the door and opened it, locked it behind them, then hurried to the end of the corridor to wait for Hoot and Charley. They appeared on time, Charley's light flashing brightly down the gallery as they approached. Joyfully they ran towards it.

"Tu-woo!" said an excited owl. "Isn't this fun? You made it O.K.?"

"Not before they led us a right, old dance," said Nero wearily. "I don't want to jig another step."

"I've blown myself clean out," added Mick, while Mack said he'd lost all the weight he'd put on the past few weeks.

The owl heard them out, then said, "No time to chat now, you folks. We have to move double-quick before the alarm's raised. The place is alive with guards. We've had the dickens of a job reaching you tonight, haven't we, Charley?"

"Affirmative," the robot said. "But guard locations are now being monitored by my radar screen. If we hurry, we'll be at base by 2030 hours as arranged."

"A most efficient robot," whispered Hoot proudly. "Quite the best I've invented. He computerises so splendidly. I don't know where he gets it from!"

Charley pretended he hadn't heard these compliments, but his light gleamed and flashed a little brighter, the nearest robots get to blushing. Then his clicking started.

"Hurry!" he said. "The aliens are waking."

Sure enough, Captain Coniophora and his crew were slowly coming back to life. He'd stopped snoring, chopped his clammy lips, then stretched hugely. Charley had opened a panel in his side which revealed a television screen. His monitor signals homed in on their cell and they saw the guard commanders stirring. One glance was enough. Charley closed his side and they took off, following him back to the Hootasub.

They weren't a second too soon. After another long yawn, the captain stared blankly around. It took him several minutes to notice his companions were fast asleep and another couple of minutes to realise there were no prisoners. "I say," he spluttered. "What under earth's happening? The feasties have gone!"

Gradually it dawned. They'd been tricked. Captain Coniophoria didn't like tricks being played on him no more than he liked losing. As a result, he grew angry.

Now when Grozzies become angry, they don't suddenly shout like us. Their anger rumbles deep inside like a volcano, taking its time to emerge. First, the veins on the captain's nose reddened, then spread to the other part of his face. In anger, he blossomed like a rose.

More and more his anger mounted till finally it burst on the inert figures of Lieutenant Monticola and Sergeants Quercina and Lacrymans, all of them blissfully unaware of what was to happen. They snored in three different keys like a tone-deaf wind trio, and the louder they snored, the more their captain's anger grew.

Finally it erupted. He stormed to where his lieutenant lay and gave him an almighty kick. "Get up! Get up!" he roared. "What's happened to the feasties?"

The lieutenant was still dreaming, dreaming he was beating the captain at Snap.

"Snap!" he said sleepily.

"What?" yelled Cerebella.

"Snap!" the other repeated from his dreamland haze.

His dream vanished under a hail of kicks. He woke, stood up, and came to attention. "I'm sorry, sir," he stammered. "I must have fallen asleep. What's happened?"

"We've been tricked!" shouted his superior. "Those two-faced feasties have given us the slip. They've escaped!"

As the captain's voice became louder, the sergeants began to awake. They looked blankly at the walls ahead for a while, but since Sergeant Merulius Lacrymans was gazing also at his two officers, and as he realised even in his dull-witted state they were very agitated, he got to his feet.

Immediately, Sergeant Quercina, whose back he'd been supporting, toppled over and lay looking through his two feet at the ceiling with his legs in the air. He couldn't understand what was happening at all, but he soon did.

"The cell key!" bawled the captain, storming to the prostrate sergeant. "Have you got the cell key?" There was no reply, so he gave the sergeant the same gentle treatment he'd given the lieutenant earlier. Quercina moved.

He searched his coat-pocket first. No key. Still lying on his back, he frantically went through his other pockets. Nothing.

"It's gone . . . disappeared!" he whimpered, falling into a fit of shudders which the captain had to kick him out of.

"Get to your feet!" ordered Captain Cerebella, and the sergeant crawled to his feet shaking like a jelly, trying to stand stiffly to attention but failing hopelessly.

Goodness knows how long the captain would have gone on shouting at his men, but gradually it dawned on him that perhaps he ought to be taking some other action, such as raising the alarm. As red as a beetroot he plodded to the door. There he stayed glued to an alarm button till a guard appeared, grumbling as he slopped down the corridor.

"What do you feasties want now?" he muttered, opening the peep-hole in the door. Great was his surprise when he saw the scarlet Captain Cerebella glaring back at him. He came to attention and saluted. "Did you ring, sir?" he asked.

"Get us out of here, you fool!" the captain barked. "The feasties have escaped!"

"Escaped?" echoed the guard. (He was particularly slow upstairs.) "But how could they get out when you're still inside?" And he scratched the back of his head in a most unmilitary way.

"Never mind about that, you idiot," roared Cerebella. "Get the spare key from the guard-room and sound the alarm. They can't have got far. They must be caught before All Gracious Mungo our King finds out. We're done for if he hears they've escaped!"

The mention of Mungo's name worked like magic on the dull guard. He didn't want to be involved in any prisoners' escape, least of all feasties. Like all Grozzies, he was terrified of Mungo and set off as fast as his legs would go.

When he'd gone, those inside had time to consider their plight, what Mungo would to do them if he found out. The captain's rage jelled to fear, and his face went white. It was catching. Before long all four stood ashen-faced by the door and shook and shook with fright.

Meanwhile, Charley led the newly freed prisoners through the maze of galleries straight to the Lonely Lake. They heard the alarm go off and sirens wailed eerily about them as they raced along.

"Alien alarm system," said Charley cheerfully. "They've discovered your escape. We must proceed with caution."

The robot dimmed his light and halted. He began clicking softly and ordered the animals to hold on to each other, as they pressed forward in the dark.

"Charley's switched to infra-red," Hoot explained. "He can see in the dark, but others can't see him. Keep close. We don't want anyone lost."

96

They moved in silence for what seemed ages until ahead they made out some kind of opening. Twice they had to retrace their steps as Grozzy guards blocked their way, but eventually the Lonely Lake came in sight, gleaming dully in the half-light of Grozzieland.

Its surface was still and menacing. So large was it, they couldn't see the further shore, though they saw distant Grozzy beams searching this way and that as they walked along its edges, or went in and out of the many tunnels leading to it.

When all was clear, Charley led them to a deserted stretch of beach. He began emitting signals to their craft. Nothing was heard for some time, then, in the half-light a black shape broke the surface and floated quietly towards them. Coming to take them on board was the Hootasub!

Chapter 11

The Lonely Lake was a sinister place. It lay in the very heart of Grozzieland, linked by underground tunnels and chambers to the Great Mere of Mellowmark many kilometres above. Through these tunnels the ancestors of the Grozzies had entered their forsaken world when they'd quit our own. The tunnels had been formed when long-gone rivers had wormed through the soft rock and disappeared. One river still flowed from the Great Mere, emptying into the Lonely Lake, but where it went from there, no one knew.

The lake was in every sense lonely. No wind ever ruffled its waters or sang across its surface. They lay still and black, oily in the dim light. Great stalactites hung like fangs waiting to impale those below. Weird rock formations grimaced like grotesque gargoyles. They hung in the darkness silent, waiting to leer down when any glimmer of light found its way in. The silence itself was oppressive, broken only by plops and drips and a distant roar which came and went like thunder. It issued from a gigantic cataract which fell many metres into the lake, as the river poured in. It was down it the Hootasub had dropped, steered skilfully by the robots inside who'd brought it safely into Grozzieland.

The strange plopping and splashes that broke the silence went on and on. They never ceased and would have driven most folks mad, but not the Grozzies. They were music to their dull ears, just as the fungi, which grew everywhere, had become delicious food to their palates. The fungi reeked of decay. Their stench was all about the place, for they grew in every nook and cranny, pale and white. And along the shores of the lake the Grozzies cultivated their favourite brands in fungus fields. These formed the main part of their diet, which they supplemented from time to time with odd animals they caught and trapped when it was dark enough for them to venture above. So long had the Grozzies eaten this food, they themselves had begun to give off the same unearthly—or, should I say 'subearthly'?—light which glimmered from the toadstools.

By this light, Nero and the others could see ghostly fish, sightless and white, which rose to the surface of the lake, puncturing it with soft rings as they searched for food. It was chill down there, and they shivered as they awaited their craft. The eeriness added to the cold. The only cheerful thing in the whole place was the Hootasub coming towards them.

None of them dared move. They all kept still and quiet behind a huge boulder near the edge of the lake. Across the other side, many Grozzies were on the prowl. Nero heard guards calling to each other as they cast their beams in all directions searching for the escaped prisoners.

"Avoid the beams," warned Charley. "The aliens have them switched to full power."

Mick, as usual, heard too late. He was peering round the boulder fascinated by all he saw, watching the distant beams of the Grozzies twinkle like fairy lights across the lake. But even at that distance they were effective. Before he could blink, they got him. He was grozzified,

The Hootasub comes to the rescue

and it wasn't until the others were about to step into the dinghy which had been sent for them that they discovered Mick was zonked out, sitting with his back to the boulder staring stonily ahead.

"What's up?" asked Mack, when he saw Mick wasn't following. "Blow me!" he exclaimed. "If the nellie ain't gone and got himself grozzified again. You can see it a mile off."

"Affirmative," said Charley. "The Grozzy beams are a mile off. Avert eyes. They're toxic." Then the robot returned and clicked smoothly as he examined Mick. "Subject should recover soon . . . only a small dose of grozzification . . . about .0003 Grozunits on the G-scale. Carry him inboard. He'll be A1 when base is reached."

Mack picked up Mick unceremoniously and hoisted him over his shoulder. "Always the same," he grumbled. "So self-willed. He just don't listen till it's too late."

They put him at the bottom of the dinghy and cast off. Within minutes they were alongside the Hootasub and clambered up to the conning-tower, lugging a very dazed Mick.

What a greeting awaited them as they climbed down the ladder. All their friends from the Great Beyond and Hedgehog Meadow were there, including little Pip. He threw up a smart salute for Mack and helped Mick to his quarters as he came unsteadily aboard. Then the submarine sank gently back into the lake, unseen and unheard.

"It is good to see you again!" said Horatio Fitzworthy, shaking hands with them in turn.

"You can't think how glad I am to see you three in one piece," said Quill. "From what Hoot told us, I imagined you'd all been . . . well, quite honestly, I imagined you'd all been eaten up."

Mack shook his hand and said wryly, "You're not alone in that. We've imagined ourselves as stews, roasts, and pies daily . . . dreamed myself magpie melange every blooming night, I have!"

They could laugh about it now, and laugh they did at the joy of being free and meeting again. "It's due to Hoot, you know, that you're free," said Horatio. "We wouldn't have had a clue how to get you out but for him."

"Not at all, not at all," said the modest owl. "All Charley's doing, I assure you." And here, Hoot gave the robot a little pat on his batteries. Charley's light beamed with pleasure and he nodded modestly, then he took himself off to see his robot friend who was navigating the sub. There he stayed in the robot room, jawing computer talk and comparing micro-systems . . . the sort of gossip all robots indulge in when they meet.

When they'd greeted the newcomers, Brushy Fox insisted they went to the galley where he could cook Nero, Mack, and Mick some decent food. "You'll need some real cooking after this toadstooly stuff they've been feeding you," he said. "I've been rustling up a little something for your arrival."

It was very crowded in the sub's galley, but the meal was splendid. For the first time in weeks, the three animals who'd been the Grozzies' prisoners ate food they liked how they liked, for the fox was a superb cook. Tight to the final button they sat back with mugs of tea when they'd finished, and after a chat the animals trooped into the chart-room to discuss the next stage of their campaign against Mungo Brown.

The room held them all comfortably, though some had to peer over the backs of others to have a decent view of the table. There, Hoot had spread the map of Grozzieland. "My friends," he began, "we now move into the final stage of Operation Mungo, thanks to the information Mick, Mack, and Nero programmed into Charley. All that remains is for us to immobilise Mungo's rockets . . . make them so that they cannot work." He added this explanation for the sake of young Pippa Vole who wasn't very good with long words like 'immobilise.' "Charley and I have studied his rockets carefully. They're quite an advanced kind. Mungo must have been working hard since we last met him. But, of course, he hasn't the resources of Owl View, nor the admirable hardworking robots who help me, so we're one or two steps ahead of him as usual." The owl gave a soft 'tu-woo' almost as if he was sorry for the alley cat. "And as usual, that dratted cat has turned what could have been good into something diabolical . . ."

"Please, Mr. Hoot," said a small voice at the owl's elbow, "what's 'dia . . .' what you said?" Pippa was beat by the owl's long words again.

"Diabolical . . . diabolical," murmured the owl, searching for another word, "well, it's . . . it's . . ."

"Devilish?" suggested Vicky Vole, trying to help out her young cousin.

"Exactly," said Hoot. "In fact, it's devilish devilish, which is twice as bad as ordinary devilish . . . and that's bad enough. O.K.?"

Pippa nodded wide-eyed.

"But not to be dismayed. Diabolical though Mungo's plans are, we have an answer, if only we could be sure where he's got his rockets."

At this point Nero coughed politely. "I think we can help you," he said. "If I may have a squint at your map for a mo, I can locate his rockets in a jiffy."

The rat came forward and after glancing at Hoot's map, plonked a finger on one of the galleries. "There," he said, "the rockets are based in the gallery in B Chamber. You see the air-shaft belonging to the old mine-workings? Well, he's extended that so that the rockets can blast up it."

"Thank you," said the owl, marking the spot with his pen. "You've got that, Charley?"

"Affirmative," replied the robot, who'd returned from his chat when the animals had gone into the chart-room.

103

"I'll check out alien-density . . ." and there began a long series of bleeps and whirrings inside the robot, as though he was chewing up metres of computer tape. Soon, all was quiet and Charley continued, ". . . alien-density intense. The rocket-base is heavily patrolled . . . manned 24 hours by 50 Grozzies. It will be impossible to reach the rockets without being spotted and grozzified. The Grozzies are armed with new Mungo automatics. They have orders to fire on sight."

A stunned silence followed. Hoot hadn't bargained on that. The problem had grown.

"Ladies and Gentlemen," he said quietly, "we must all put on our thinking-caps."

And so the animals began their collective think and thunk hard.

Suddenly, Nero began dancing up and down, rather like the jig he'd performed for the Grozzy commanders. "I have it!" he yelled.

The others looked hard, as if he'd picked up something catching.

"Nick's whistle! It works wonders on the Grozzies. When they hear it, they'll begin dancing. They can't help themselves," he explained.

"Like the Pied Piper the Humanfolk once had," said the little vole.

"Exactly," said Nero. "If we can get Mick into the gallery, he can pipe out the guards, then you and Charley can go to work on the rockets."

"You've saved the day," said Hoot, "just like you did when we captured Mungo before."

The rat looked modestly at his toes, then laughed. "When Mick starts to play his whistle, we too can play . . . play with the Grozzies like toys. They can't resist him. He's the grozzificator of Grozzies!"

"It'll be a real pleasure," commented Mick, taking out his whistle. "I've suffered enough myself at their eyes . . .

now *I'll* call the tune for a change. I'll mickify the lot of 'em."

At this point Police-cadet Pip raised his hand. Horatio invited him to speak, and the fieldmouse said, "I don't want to seem negative . . . but have you thought that the Grozzies might grozzify Mick first? He can't play his whistle if he's grozzified."

"A good question, my lad," said Sergeant Mack. "I'm glad to see some of my training has gone in. Always ask yourself the problems first, I says, before you comes up with any answers. Well, Mick, what d'you have to say? What's the answer? How will you stop yourself being grozzified? You knows you're allergic to Grozzies."

Mick looked blank. He hadn't thought of that. The smile of triumph had gone from his face and all he could murmur was, "I don't know."

Charley began clicking and flashing his light. There was something he wanted to say. Hoot turned and said, "Yes, Charley? Have you a suggestion?"

"Affirmative . . . sun-glasses. Polaroid. My rearward computer has come up with those. There are sun-glasses stowed in the medical room. They'll neutralise Grozzy rays," said Charley.

"Tu-woo, of course," exclaimed the owl. "There's your answer, Pip."

"Thank you," said the fieldmouse.

"Then go and collect them," ordered Mack. That always happened when Pip came up with answers. He finished up doing the work!

Pip toddled off for Mick's glasses and Hoot said they should get some shut-eye before they went ashore again. But before they retired, Rachel Water-Rat had them synchronise watches, just to make sure they all woke up together three hours later. She was a stickler for good time-keeping and being at rendezvous at exactly the right time.

105

And three hours, fifteen minutes later four dinghies left the Hootasub and paddled silently to the shore. The raid on the rocket-base had begun.

Chapter 12

I didn't really want to describe what happened when the four Grozzy commanders were hauled before Mungo to explain how their prisoners had escaped. The scene was almost too painful for me to relate.

Mungo was livid. He was about as wild as a cat can get. His glasses got darker and his voice got hotter. Its sloshy sound hissed like water on the boil. He growled and spat most horribly. He couldn't stay still a moment but paced back and forth across the royal audience chamber. When Captain Coniophora reported the prisoners had gone, he and his men were immediately stripped of all rank and made prisoners. They wore the very chains Nero, Mick, and Mack had worn hours earlier.

Mungo paced so fiercely his crown slipped to the back of his head, hanging at a dizzy angle. He snarled and ranted as he strode, twisting and turning the rings on his paws, terrifying all the Grozzy bodyguards, who lined the chamber flattened against the wall with fear.

"The idiots!" he yelled for the umpteenth time. "Letting the over-earthlings escape from their cell! Why haven't they been caught? They must be down here somewhere . . . no one can get out of this place." He paused, as if a new idea had entered his mind, and addressed his corps of guards. "Catch 'em and you can have 'em . . . grilled for your suppersies!" he said.

For the first time in hours, the guards relaxed. They peeled themselves off the walls and smiled thinly, smacking their lips.

"And the rat . . . we'll have him specially garnished as an entrée with your favourite toadstools," he added.

More lip-smacking dripped from the walls together with a certain damp shuffling. Mungo could stir the Grozzy imagination and they were keen to be off after their prey. But before they could leave, a court official called out, "The prisoners you ordered to be brought have arrived, All Gracious Mungo!"

Into the chamber slouched the erstwhile guard commanders, heavily guarded, led by ex-Captain Coniophora Cerebella. They had already been punished severely, but Mungo liked to go on punishing to work out his anger.

The chains they wore shook and jangled, as they shivered before him. A gummy tear welled in the eye of Cerebella and plopped to the floor. They were all much larger and taller than Mungo, yet they trembled.

"Tell me again how they gave you the slip," he ordered savagely. "Listening to you tell it keeps me on the boil . . . and when I'm on the boil I like to bubble over and scald!"

His words drew a long sob deep inside the former captain. His comrades in chains blubbered openly, so much so they soon stood in little pools of tears.

Mungo remained silent, gaining some grain of satisfaction from their fearful appearance. Then he started raging once more, and his guards flattened themselves to the wall. So angry was he, his crown began to jig on his head and threatened to part company with him any moment.

"Do you realise that if any of those prisoners had found their way to my rockets, the whole project, years of work would have been ruined? None of us would get to the world above. We'd all grow into toadstools . . . into giant Fly Agarics!" His voice trailed off as his words sank in. Hisses of fear swept the walls. His guards trembled. Then he went quiet, and when Mungo went quiet, something particularly nasty had surfaced in his mind. Someone was in for it . . . and all there knew who.

The cat strolled to his throne, adjusting his crown to a more becoming angle. His gown trailed evilly, and he looked very, very malevolent. On reaching the throne, he swept his gown behind to keep his tail in order, then sat down. His fingers drummed on the golden arms of his seat, till the half-light made his jewels glint and flash like spurts of flame. He started smiling . . . a slow sort of smile which grew in malice. Then he broke into a soft chuckle. His wicked scheme had at last taken shape.

He purred quietly in a satisfied way and said finally, "Yes, that's what I'll do. I'll send you lot into space. You'll have a free ride on my rockets. You'll have a close-up view of the sun and moon. You'll see them blown to bits as you join them yourselves!"

"Oh, Most Gracious Majesty," wailed Poria Monticola hurling himself at Mungo's feet, wetting the cat's tootsies with his tears. "Spare me! Not the rocketsies!"

"They're about the only things which can blow sense into you," growled the cat, kicking him away to avoid wetting his gown.

Then arose a great rattling of ironmongery as the quartet lifted their chains and pleaded for their lives. The bedlam would have gone on longer, till Mungo sent them below, but he didn't get that far. A strange noise, a thin, piping sound came from the galleries outside. It came closer and closer . . . the sound of music, the sound of a jib being played on a tin-whistle.

The first note halted the Grozzies' grovelling. Those lining the walls relaxed, dropped away and slowly began to jog in time with the music, rocking from side to side. Their eyes became glazed, and dreamy smiles drifted onto their faces. Those on the floor dried up, then stood and rattled their chains in a heavy dance. They'd been mickified.

Mungo stared in disbelief. His fat smile of satisfaction thinned to open-mouthed amazement, as he watched his guards shuffle off one by one in the direction of the music.

"Come back! Come back!" he commanded, but to no avail. Within minutes he was deserted. Even his prisoners had gone, weighed as they were with chains, crashing and clanging after the mysterious music like so many pieces of hardware dropping from shelves.

Mungo was quite alone and sat mystified till it dawned on him his kingdom was under threat. It had been invaded. "The Great Beyonders! They've arrived!" he gasped, and in that instant he leapt from his throne, racing for the rocket-base. Never had he run so fast, yet he was held up all the way by hordes of Grozzies under the spell of music, all jogging lustily down every corridor and tunnel. Drawn by Mick's whistle like toads to water.

But at last Mungo arrived, minus his crown. His robe was torn and muddy. His glasses steamy and slipping down his nose. And as he turned into the tunnel which led to the rockets, there stood Hoot and Charley next to them, right next to the two, huge rockets.

Mungo drew up short. "You!" he shouted. "I might have guessed it!"

"Tu-woo," replied Hoot. "You guessed right. Meet my chief assistant, Charley. He knows a great deal about you already, Mungo. Indeed probably more than you know about yourself." And the owl smiled most amiably which infuriated the feline more.

"Mere computer prattle," sneered Mungo. "Where are the rest of your gang?"

"Five minutes away . . ." began Hoot.

110

"Correction, sir. Four point two minutes," said Charley, whose feeling for chronometry was modelled on Rachel Water-Rat.

"You see, we work to more exact timings than yourself," said Hoot. "You know, Mungo, my good man, it's no use. You can't win. If I were you I'd do a bunk and forget all about this business. Go into something more catlike . . . such as, well, how about a creamery? Less trouble than a kingdom."

Mungo ignored him. He rushed to a control-panel near the rockets and flicked a switch. He'd fired the motors. There was a hot roar as the firing mechanism started up, followed by a mighty rumble when fuel injected into the engines. Finally, with an ear-shattering blast the rockets took off. They rose slowly from their pads, gaining speed all the time as they slipped up the shaft into the night and away to the emptiness of space.

The rockets cleared the mines and were speeding away when the Great Beyonders rushed onto the pad. Coughing and spluttering through the exhaust fumes, Big Bill Badger saw Mungo, and before the cat could bolt, he'd collared him and held him dangling at the end of his huge paw.

Mungo kicked a while then hung limp. "It's no use," he sneered. "Your fate is sealed. Do with me what you will. You're too late. The whole earth will be plunged into darkness when my rockets hit the moon and sun. You won't stop then reaching their targets now!"

"Negative," said a cool voice by the badger. Charley had trundled up to look at Mungo more closely. His light flashed brightly. He was evidently pleased about something.

"What?" shouted the cat, swinging round under Bill's grip.

"Negative," the robot repeated. "I've re-orientated the rockets' flight-plan. The retro-engines will fire shortly and

111

bring the rockets round so that they'll collide in space . . .
ten point seven eight four kilometers up from the surface of the earth exactly. They'll explode harmlessly. Please
to observe the scanning panel. Impact is in twenty point
nought nought five seconds."

All eyes flicked to the scanning panel. The rockets could
clearly be seen and for a time they flew on parallel courses.
Then there was a slight puff of exhaust smoke and the
two flight-paths quite noticeably started to converge. They
were on collision courses.

"Ten, nine, eight, seven, six, five, four, three, two, one
. . . zero!" counted Charley.

Right before them on the panel a huge flash lit up the
screen. Down the ventilation hatches a few seconds later
came muffled bangs from out in space. And on the earth
above, countless children saw the best firework display
of their lives. Coloured lights went this way and that, burn-
ing out in the blackness overhead. At length, a profound
silence returned and the moon and stars shone down as
peacefully as ever.

Deep under the earth, silence reigned, too. The screen
went blank and all turned to Mungo Brown. The badger
put him down and he stood limply, shrinking into his
bedraggled robe looking glumly at the empty screen.

"I said you ought to have done a bunk while you could,
Mungo," said Hoot. "But it's too late now."

And too late it was. Mungo was stripped of his gown
and crown. He became a nobody again . . . and didn't like
it one bit. To be simply a good-for-nothing alley cat hurt
him most of all. He hadn't a friend in the world because
he didn't want friends, only servants or slaves. He could
share nothing except his own bad character with those
like himself. He was put under lock and key again till
the Animalfolk decided to let him go, for in their world
nobody is imprisoned long.

As for the Grozzies, lacking a leader and knowing what was in store for them if they stayed underground, they made their way up to the world above. You see, music revived what spark of decency was still alive. Of course, for some considerable time they had to wear dark glasses till their one eye got used to the sun, but Mick's music certainly charmed them to higher things. They discovered by degrees they could see more clearly in the world of light and air. They saw how green the grass was, how beautifully coloured were the flowers. They looked for hours at the blue sky and white clouds, the moon in a star-filled sky. Most wonderful of all, they saw the magic of the dawn and sunset for the very first time and were filled with awe.

Gone went their hatred of other people. Gone, too, went their hurtful power of grozzifying. With it happened the strangest thing of all. Their one dull eye began to change. It was as if with only one eye they couldn't take in enough of the wonderful world they'd just entered. Slowly over the years, their solitary eye began to widen, then to divide in two. It moved down their faces along either side of their noses till two eyes were formed again just like our own.

They drifted about the Animalfolk world for some time living decent, civilised lives, until it was time for them to return to Humanfolk Land where they really belonged. In due course they found their way to some islands called the Britty Isles and were known as Grozzybrits at first. Later, however, they were called Grossbritannien by their neighbours. They still live quietly if rather eccentrically there and are thought rather comical by the people over the water, who keep a friendly eye on them.

The animals returned to their homes in the Great Beyond, Mellowmark, and Domusland, full of tales and long winter yarns. Quill, in fact, spent the whole of the following winter up-dating Dink Dormouse about what had happened, while Mick and Mack resumed their duties at the station aided by P.C. Pip Fieldmouse, who passed his police exams with honours. I ought to mention the Black Wood Shire police station still resembles a market garden . . . but they don't grow mushrooms any more.

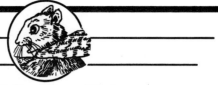

Your Nature Diary

_____

_____

_____

_____

_____

_____

_____

_____

_____

_____

_____

_____

_____

_____

_____

_____

Join the
Quill Hedgehog Club

Quill and his friends invite you to join their Quill Hedgehog Club and receive the latest exciting news from Hedgehog Corner.

When you become a member of the club, you will receive a *membership certificate*, a *Hedgehog Club badge*, and *Quill's Club Newsletter*, which is issued four times a year.

You will be among the very first to learn about Quill and his friends' newest adventures and their battles to protect the environment.

To join, just send your name and address and $10.00 to:

> Quill Hedgehog
> Hedgehog Corner
> Fair View, Old Coppice
> Lyth Bank
> Shrewsbury
> Shropshire
> England SY3 0BW

from John Muir Publications

The Quill Hedgehog Adventure Series

*I*n our first series of green fiction for young readers, Quill Hedgehog, an ardent environmentalist, and his animalfolk friends battle such foes as the villainous alley cat Mungo Brown, the Wasteland rats, and the Grozzies.

Quill's Adventures in the Great Beyond
Book One
John Waddington-Feather
5½" × 8½", 96 pages, $5.95 paper

Quill's Adventures in Wasteland
Book Two
John Waddington-Feather
5½" × 8½", 132 pages, $5.95 paper

Quill's Adventures in Grozzieland
Book Three
John Waddington-Feather
5½" × 8½", 132 pages, $5.95 paper

The Extremely Weird Series

*F*ew things of the imagination are as amazing or as weird as the wonders that Mother Nature produces, and that's the idea behind our Extremely Weird series. Each title is filled with full-size, full-color photographs and descriptions of the extremely weird thing depicted.

Extremely Weird Bats
Text by Sarah Lovett
8½" × 11", 48 pages, $9.95 paper

Extremely Weird Frogs
Text by Sarah Lovett
8½" × 11", 48 pages, $9.95 paper

Extremely Weird Spiders
Text by Sarah Lovett
8½" × 11", 48 pages, $9.95 paper

Extremely Weird Primates
Text by Sarah Lovett
8½" × 11", 48 pages, $9.95

Extremely Weird Reptiles
Text by Sarah Lovett
8½" × 11", 48 pages, $9.95

The Kids' Environment Series

*T*he titles in this series, all of which are printed on recycled paper, examine the environmental issues and opportunities that kids will face during their lives. They suggest ways young people can become involved and thoughtful citizens of planet Earth.

Rads, Ergs, and Cheeseburgers
The Kids' Guide to Energy and the Environment
Bill Yanda
Illustrated by Michael Taylor
7" × 9", 108 pages, two-color illustrations, $12.95 paper

The Kids' Environment Book
What's Awry and Why
Anne Pedersen
Illustrated by Sally Blakemore
7" × 9", 192 pages, two-color illustrations, $13.95 paper
For Ages 10 and Up

The Indian Way
Learning to Communicate with Mother Earth
Gary McLain
Paintings by Gary McLain
Illustrations by Michael Taylor
7" × 9", 114 pages, two-color illustrations, $9.95 paper

The Kidding Around Series

*W*ith our Kidding Around series, we are making the world more accessible to young travelers. All the titles listed below are 64 pages and $9.95 except for *Kidding Around the National Parks of the Southwest* and *Kidding Around Spain*, which are 108 pages and $12.95.

"A combination of practical information, vital statistics, and historical asides."
—New York Times

Kidding Around Atlanta
Kidding Around Boston
Kidding Around Chicago
Kidding Around the Hawaiian Islands
Kidding Around London
Kidding Around Los Angeles
Kidding Around the National Parks of the Southwest
Kidding Around New York City
Kidding Around Paris
Kidding Around Philadelphia
Kidding Around San Diego
  (Available September 1991)
Kidding Around San Francisco
Kidding Around Santa Fe
Kidding Around Seattle
Kidding Around Spain
  (Available September 1991)
Kidding Around Washington, D.C.

Kids Explore America's Hispanic Heritage

*W*ritten by kids, for kids. Topics covered range from history, festivals, cuisine, and dress to heroes, mythology, music, and language.

Edited by Judy Cozzens
7" × 9", 112 pages, $7.95 paper

KIDDING AROUND

SPAIN

A YOUNG PERSON'S GUIDE

KIDDING AROUND

San Diego

A YOUNG PERSON'S GUIDE TO THE CITY

RUTH LUHRS
ILLUSTRATED BY MARY LAMBERT